CORE-UPTION

PROFESSOR SUE-C

Core-Uption
Copyright © 2022 by Professor Sue-C

All rights reserved. No part of this publication may be reproduced, distributed, or transmitted in any form or by any means, including photocopying, recording, or other electronic or mechanical methods, without the prior written permission of the author, except in the case of brief quotations embodied in critical reviews and certain other non-commercial uses permitted by copyright law.

ISBN
978-1-956529-58-6 (Paperback)
978-1-956529-57-9 (eBook)

CONTENTS

CHAPTER 1

WEAK END WARRIORS

Josh Durbin
June 7, 2014

9 AM- It's the first morning of summer break and I'm sitting in the kitchen with my brother, Avery, and his girlfriend Jules. They are upset because they must stay with me until my grandfather picks me up. My grandfather and I are going camping. I hope to fulfill the requirements for two Boy Scout badges. Avery and Jules are leaving this morning for a nature camp in Big Bear. Daichi, Jules' twin brother is here. He is going to drive them and their baggage to the high school where they will meet their group.

Blah, blah, blah....

This is what I wrote to turn into my English teacher when I got back from summer break. This is what I was really thinking...

9 AM- Halfway through summer break! (Yep, I procrastinated and now I have four weeks of journaling to do before school starts). I get to go fishing with my grandfather. This should be a reason for celebration but here I sit at the kitchen table with Acne Face Avery and his girlfriend, Jelly Butt Jules. Neither of these nicknames has any validity. I think Avery has had two zits in his life, but just calling him Acne Face Avery will send him running to the bathroom mirror to examine every inch of his neck and face. Jules is barely five feet and weighs about the same as my Manx cat. The name gets her riled up and stammering, which is the intent.

Three boxes of cereal and I end up with dust. Looking down, a few intact pieces of Captain Crunch float in the bowl that I had primed with milk in anticipation, of course there are bran flakes left. There are always bran flakes left. The two of them sit crunching spoonful after spoonful of perfectly formed Captain Crunch and Strawberry Mini Wheats. Laughing, they each raised their eyes toward me as they provocatively placed the hard, crunchy cereal into their mouths. They are waiting for me to say something, but I refuse to give them that satisfaction.

I get up and go to the freezer, aha! Toaster Strudel! So, take that Acne Face and Jiggling Jelly Butt! I reach in and....empty...someone put an empty box back in the freezer! Arg, I would cuss but my mom might find this regardless of where I hid it, even if I threw it away, even if I shredded it, my mother would find the paper...so no cussing here!

Rummaging through the freezer produced two waffles that were joined like Siamese twins, and it took almost as much effort for me to separate them as it took the doctors on Discovery to separate real Siamese Twins. After exerting efforts, I managed to separate them intact enough to survive toasting. Not a perfect breakfast, but frostbitten waffles are better than frosted dust floating in now warm milk. The hoarders looked up as I put the waffles in the toaster. I had been stealthy about the surgical separation. Avery noticed and raised an eyebrow in covetous envy, "Hey, where'd ya git the waffles? "No, fair!" He stammered.

"Are there anymore?" Jelly Butt demanded.

"Nope, but I'll trade a bowl of cereal for the waffles." I propositioned, attempting to appear aloof and detached from the outcome.

They looked at one another. Jiggle spoke first, "Is there syrup?"

"Of course," I say with an air of indignation.

"I'll trade you." She slid over her practically full bowl of my favorite cereal of all time, Captain Crunch. The cereal swayed in the milk as I cupped my hands to stop it from sliding off the edge of the table and into my lap.

"Hey, watch it!" I snapped as the bowl came to an abrupt halt, milk sloshing over onto the table. Lifting her spoon out of the bowl, I sent the spoon sliding back to her, "Ewww!" was accompanied by a look of exaggerated disdain.

Ignoring my indignation, she demanded. "Gimme the waffles Wienie!"

"Not til I git a new spoon!" Negotiations at the kitchen table are tough.

"Dweeb!" she retorted as she pushed her chair back, leaning and reaching with her right hand into the drawer that held the flatware. My mother insisted that we call it flatware since it wasn't silverware. Silverware needs to be polished and is stolen by lecherous relatives or servants. We had no servants, but we did have some lecherous relatives. So, I guess it is good that we didn't have silverware.

"Here, Dork Breath." She snapped as she sent the spoon careening across the table. (Um and this really is an insult...well if you know what a dork is... which...naw...she has no idea... or maybe she does.)

"Don't you guys need to get going to your granola crunching tree hugging campfire fest?" This lit a fire under both of them.

Their words dodged in and out of sync. Scrambled in the mix was "You booger faced baboon, you wouldn't know the first thing about..." Daichi's roar interrupted the frenzy.

"Hey, you guys!!!" He hollered as he emerged from the hall. We all stopped and looked at him. He tugged on Jules short black ponytail that looked like a cosmetic brush sticking out of her head. Jules turned and swiped at him. Daichi dodged her in his cool jock- like manner.

"What Cha got to eat?" He half asked and more demanded. We all looked at him like he had been beamed down from an alien spaceship. Had he not heard us fighting over the scraps of food we could find? He was such a dufus!

Daichi looked like a total oaf, and he used that to his advantage. Though he and Jules were twins he was the direct opposite of Jules. He was six foot three and solid like a brick wall. He was quick and agile, a top athlete. His high school accomplishments had the town talking. This was his senior year and the rumors that he had at least five universities offering full ride scholarships elevated him to celebrity status. His 3.85 GPA was never talked about and Daichi was fine with that. He wanted to be known for his brawn and not his brain. Playing the dumb jock had paid off. Before major tests he had a rotating schedule of girls eager to tutor him. Once he passed, he had the opportunity to celebrate with these girls. He was the guy every girl wanted, and every guy wanted to be. To me he was a Neanderthal breath. Wow, I know a whole lot of not so flattering facts about three of the most popular high school seniors, this must be worth something, somehow. I was brought back to the present.

"Plenty of food," Avery said, smirking, as he pointed to the empty boxes of cereal. Daichi greedily eyed the boxes, "Been workin' out for, what time is it?"

"8:43" Jules mumbled, syrup oozing from the saturated waffle filling her mouth. With the pad of her index finger, she swooped it back through her parted lips. Swallowing, she repeated. "8:43, well 44 now."

Humorously Daichi pretended to calculate the hours, producing a pregnant pause. He looked up to the ceiling as if there was a calculator and scratch pad up there, drawing in the air with his index finger. His eyes squinted; his fingers moved as he carried numbers over. Finally, he stammered. "Since, well, early this morning."

"You are too much," Avery laughed. We all responded to his humor which made him unmentionably happy.

He shouted, "Hell week starts today!" FOOTBALL!" Flexing his arm produced a solid round bulge the size of a healthy grapefruit. My own bicep tightened, only to resemble a half-buried ping pong ball. I consoled myself with the anticipation of a testosterone filled puberty, which being fourteen meant I had hope for seven years of hormonal saturation left. Jules had noticed me flexing and began shaking her head and laughing, "Yeah, you can dream Squirt."

My relaxed arm fell to my side. I shot her my iciest stare through squinted eyes. Silently I consoled myself, none of you are sponsored snow boarders. None of you are in honors math. None of you won the regional spelling bee. Well, none of you care about the spelling bee. I looked at the three of them as coconspirators against my confidence.

Then it dawned on me, Hell week was in August, and this was April. He was still playing baseball. "Hey Daichi, Hell week isn't until August and it was July."

"If I say it starts now it starts NOW!!! Hell Week!" Daichi shouted into my ear.

Pulling away from him I asked desperately, "When is grandpa pickin me up to go fishin?" I asked no one and everyone. No response. "What time is grandpa picking me up?" I repeated loudly. No one acknowledged me. I turned my attention back to my coveted Captain Crunch.

Daichi lifted one box of cereal after the other, shaking vigorously, "Funny, you are a real comedian." Directed at Avery, who smirked as he shoveled a spoonful of cereal into his mouth. And comedian comes out as CO M E DI AN. This wasn't for emphasis; it was like he was sounding the word out to say it.

Like I did in the spelling bee. He was such a doofus! A doofus that appeared to have the whole world at his feet or at least the West end of our little desert town.

"Okay, So, you don't have to do the dumb act here, we all know you are dumb for real." Avery smiled smugly and fist butted Jules. Daichi continued his search for food.

"After you drive us to the high school you have to take Dad to work," Jules said to Daichi.

"You guys babysittin' this dweeb," Daichi pointed to me offhandedly.

"I don't need babysittin," I venomously retorted, "Especially by a big, lobotomized lummox like you!"

"Why you little...." Daichi reached his arm out to grab me. I stood up like David facing Goliath. Jules- she is intervening on my behalf so I will refrain from name calling- stepped between us. She grabbed his collar, reaching as she stood on her tip toes, she pulled him down to eye level.

"Let me just…" Daichi stammered before Jules, gained his full attention.

"Reealy, So, reeealy, you are going thump on nerdly here?" She nodded her head in my direction. Daichi slowly stood up, Jules gradually let go of his collar.

"Ah, fooled you all," Daichi laughed, "If I sneezed that chump would blow away. I would never hurt little Joshie."

His tone made my blood boil, but not enough to keep things going. I would accept my reprieve from a dreaded fate gracefully.

"And YOU!" Jules turned on me, pulling me close to her by my shirt collar "Stop being such a jerk!"

I turned to Avery. He reached over and cuffed me upside my head, as I gave my most innocent, "I didn't do anything?" look. Avery gave a look of annoyance every younger brother knows "you are a walking ad for birth control" was conveyed without a word spoken.

"I don't need you guys here, just go, Grandpa will get here soon" I stated, equally as agitated, "I'll be fine by myself."

"No, mom said I can't leave until Grandpa picks you up." Avery said in his special big brother voice. Mom, mom and dad, decided to take advantage of being kidless for a week and went on a cruise. So, I was stuck here with them until Grandpa comes.

I continued pleading my case so they wouldn't think I needed them here, "I won't say a word. Grandpa won't snitch."

Avery shook his head, "Grandpa should be here in fifteen minutes, just chill."

Tipping my bowl to drink the milk from the cereal bowl, I got up, tossed the plastic bowl in the sink and went onto the back porch where Jules had been standing.

Shaking his head, Avery joined Jules on the porch too. Avery had once again become Acne Face, as he slipped his arm around Jiggle's waist, YUCK! Lobotomy Brain rolled his eyes toward Jules and turned his attention back to the fridge. He emerged with a dry piece of pizza which had been lost in the back for who knows how long. I went back to writing what would turn into my journal assignment, wondering what she would think if I wrote about my unfiltered life.

"So whatcha writin' beanpole?" I could smell the stale pizza on his breath.

"I'm writing a journal for English class. My teacher, Ms. Turner, wants us to write about summer break." I said without looking up. In our small middle school the teachers taught all the grades of their subject. So, I would have her next year for English again. Which was good. She always smelled like a bouquet of flowers.

"You ought to hang with me and you could write some real good stuff!" Daichi said while putting way too much effort in grinding the cardboard like pizza with his molars on the left side of his mouth.

"Yep, I could show you a thing or two." Slapping me on the back for emphasis, his heavy hand connecting, covering the whole of my back with a thud. My body reverberated, I coughed. The shaking continued!

"What the @#& was that!" (Still no cuss words, Mom). Daichi asked, "An earthquake?"

As I ducked under the table, I realized that it was the sharp jolting and the rolling wave of an earthquake, it felt like the house was being pulled. I said this all out loud. Daichi, who was under the table, said under his breath, "Google Geek."

Avery was standing in the doorway, "Wha @&%@!"*

The house began to teeter. I looked around, Avery, and Daichi, Jules! Where was Jules!?

The back part of the house plunged sharply, there was a blood curdling scream! Jules! Avery was holding white knuckled onto the doorframe. Daichi and I got out from under the table, crossing the kitchen toward the deck. Daichi pulled Avery who went sliding across the kitchen floor as the house lunged in the other direction. I held onto Daichi's waist as I looked to see that both Jules and the deck were gone!

CHAPTER 2

SHAKEN AND STIRRED

Avery, Daichi, and I, stood on the threshold leading from the kitchen to the back deck. The deck was gone! GONE!!!.... the backyard was gone.... and.... Jules was.... GONE!!!! The shaking and pulling was an implosion, a deep sinkhole had engulfed our whole backyard. A dark abyss remained, rocks were sliding in, and we never heard indications that they ever hit bottom.

"C'mon, I need your help!" Avery hollered to Daichi who stood staring in horror, melding with shock. His sister had been swallowed up by the earth, his mouth gaping and tears welled. Avery hollered again, "C'mon, both of you! Jules, she needs our help!" Avery pointed directly down from the threshold. We joined him. Our gaze followed his pointing finger to the dirt wall created from the implosion.

There, jutting out under the threshold was a two by four secured joist. Precariously Jules dangled from it, being held only by the hood of her hoodie. My heart was in my throat as I watched her struggle, feet dangling, her arms stretched over her head reaching to grasp the splintered wood. She struggled to dig her heels into the wall of the sink hole to push herself up high enough to grab onto the board. The soil was too soft for her to gain a foothold.

Jules squirmed. Using every ounce of energy, she had to reach above and grab the board. "Help," she groaned and grunted, gasping unlike the fem fatals in the movies, "Get something to pull me up!" The three of us remained helplessly looking on. "NOW! Move your #$%@ butts!" (No, she did not say butts.) Her fury fueled her efforts, and her left hand reached the board, her fingers bled as she wrapped them around the splintering board, swinging her right hand up, nearly overlapping her left. Her hood remained stuck to the end of the board.

The sight had mesmerized us as it looked supernatural. We stood gawking until Jules' not so delicate demand assaulted our ears for the second time. "Go get some rope or something to get me out of here! Now! You @#$%^ Now!" She struggled, reaffirming her grasp. Her feet had kicked a lip in the wall, and she was able to balance some of her weight, providing a slight reprieve for her. Oh, did I feel awful for the Jelly Butt comments.

Avery took control, "Go get the rope from the pantry, and dad's belt! HURRY!" I scrambled, having a hard time gaining traction, my muscles were numb with endorphins. My legs felt heavy and unresponsive, but I finally got to where I needed to be, returning with the requested items.

Taking the rope and belt, with the skills he learned as an Eagle Scout, Avery manufactured a makeshift rescue harness. We became a human pulley system, each grabbing onto the waist of the one in front. Daichi held the rope, wrapped around his forearm. Avery held his right hand around Daichi's waist, with his left he extended the loose length of the rope tethered to the fastened belt. Jules remained still as he extended the harness down beyond her feet. After several attempts, and Jules' hands beginning to slip, he looped the harness over her feet and pulled it up the length of her outstretched body. As it rose under her armpits Jules would need to let go of the board and immediately grab the rope while keeping her upper arms tight to her torso. Like some daredevil act without a net. My stomach flopped at the thought.

In a voice that did not bely his calm exterior, Avery related to Jules what she needed to do and then asked if she was ready. After what seemed an eternity of silence, in a voice firm with resolve, Jules said, "Okay." We steadied ourselves. We waited for her to let go of the board. After taking several deep breaths she glanced heavenward and let go. Reaching out for the rope as it pulled the harness up, along her torso, she executed the instructions with perfection.

Adrenaline rushed through my body, and I am sure through everyone else's as we pulled. The hood of the sweatshirt, lifted from the board with little resistance, falling onto her upper back. With syncopated heaves, we pulled her up. When her feet were even with the board, she used it as support to push herself up, making the harness fit against the middle of her back and not directly under her arms.

As she pushed, the board cracked and broke away from the joist, dirt and rocks added to the debris as the board swirled into the darkness. We pulled with all the power that we had, and Jules was lifted to the surface.

With one final heave, Jules' feet met the threshold of the door. We all fell back as the tension was released, landing with a thud on the kitchen floor, Daichi's mass came hunkering down on me. Jules was pulled down onto the heap.

The house lurched and began teetering. Without a word we scrambled to our feet, Jules agilely stepped out of the harness. joining us as we ran. The house continued to teeter. With pictures and knick-knacks flying, ordinary household items became projectiles. The refrigerator was jerked loose. It rolled as the house tilted. We dodged our way through the house, which had turned into an obstacle course. The refrigerator seemed to be seeking escape from certain doom. Daichi was nearly overtaken by it but was saved by the solid door jamb between the kitchen and the dining room. When the fridge hit the frame, the beam buckled, and the plaster cracked on the dining room side of the wall. Daichi looked over his shoulder when he heard the thud, he was tripped by the ottoman rolling with each tilt of the house.

Bruised and battered, he rose and regained his stride, the house tilting toward the front side assisted us as we made a hasty exit through the front door. Daichi was the last to spill out. When his last step was taken onto the front lawn, the house balanced waveringly for a slight moment. Then like a teeter totter being abandoned by the anchor person, it rose on end and with an ominous creak.... the house's last breath, it rattled and roared, groaning as boards pulled apart, into the ever-growing abyss. We sat in exhausted heaps on the lawn, all too stunned to speak, then Daichi began to sob. This caused the rest of us to react. Avery went over and held Jules, who was staring blankly at her oozing and painful hands. I heaved up the coveted Captain Crunch.

I looked up, just in time to protect myself from a projectile that the falling house had vomited out. My Avengers backpack slammed into my forearms which were folded in front of my face. It knocked the wind out of me. As I sat gasping for air, I felt the earth move under my butt! Sliding like sand being pulled by waves as they return to the sea. I screamed, yes, I screamed...like a .... like a child...like a little child.... Daichi and Jules looked over at me, our eyes connected. I sunk lower. Then I could see in their faces that the same thing was happening to them. "@#%$!" Jules exclaimed.

Daichi looked up, his face wet, snot running from his nose, he wiped it on his forearm and stood up to intervene on our behalf. Too late! He lost his footing in his attempt to stand and was toppled over with us. This new sinkhole imploded. What we experienced could not be described as falling, the surface of the earth collapsed, and we went with it!

Cocooned in what was once our lawn we fell spinning for what seemed an eternity. In reality it was probably about twenty-seconds. The grass cushioned our landing and provided us a pocket of air. We had fallen into some kind of cave and the remaining dirt-lawn mixture completely enveloped us. We were trapped. The grass wrapped around us, agitating my allergies and all our skin.

My eyes began feeling puffy and the blades of grass etched my skin with tiny red welts. We squirmed attempting to find a spot for each of us in this inverted turf bubble. Elbows met noses, and knees bent, legs stretched as we struggled to settle in. Finally, the movement ended. Daichi spoke first, "Avery?" Avery responded with a muffled, "Yeah."

Daichi inquired, "Jules?" Jules replied with a deep sigh, "Yeah." Daichi inquired one more time. "Josh?" I responded, "Yeah." To break the tension, I inquired, "Daichi?" Daichi responded, "Duh!"

"Well, I guess we are all accounted for," Avery added, "Is everyone all right? I mean is anyone hurt?"

"Except for itching from the grass, I am fine." Responded Daichi.

In a nasal tone I responded, "I'm itchy and my throat is feeling like it's closing." Wheezing followed this short statement, my lungs burnt as I took another breath.

"OMG, we need to get him out of here," it was Jules. With that they all started pushing against the grass encasement. I could hear Avery saying, "Oh poop, oh poop, oh poop." All I could do was concentrate on breathing. Daichi ripped off a piece of his shirt for me to hold over my nose and mouth as a filter. "I know this isn't much, but hopefully it will help a little, Josh." I was really worried now. He didn't even call me a derogatory name, not even Joshie. I knew we were in serious trouble now!

With these thoughts running through my head, making me realize the gravity of the situation, I stayed as still as I could listen to them strategize. Each was going to attempt a different way to escape our predicament. As they worked, I began to wonder what we would be escaping to.

Avery deduced that the implosion would have caused the grass to fold over onto itself, therefore, he hoped to find a flap which could be separated. Jules was convinced that by pushing on the walls of grass, it would unroll, the sides pulling away from the seam that Avery was looking for. Daichi opted for cutting us out with his deluxe Buck knife, the blade was four inches long. I visualized the turf sold at Home Depot; the full thickness was about three to four inches. I would bet on this over the other options. It was becoming increasingly difficult for me to breathe. The wheezing intensified. I concentrated on filling my lungs as full as I could before exhaling. My breaths became increasingly shallow and I began losing consciousness.

Jules kicked something out of her way as she edged her way around the dome, pushing against the wall. The object tumbled over and rested near my right shoulder. It was bulky and about the size of a folded bed pillow. I reached over and felt a familiar shape, my nails scratched the vinyl surface. Straps trapped my hand as I pulled back from it.

It was my backpack! The Avengers had come to my rescue. If I had not become so weakened by the lack of oxygen, I would have expressed the joy and relief in my heart. My mother had replenished my supplies just that morning. A source of regular arguments between us. She put Kleenex, lip balm, hand sanitizer, three water bottles, vitamins, a box of granola bars, cough drops, an orange, peanut M&M's, a box with six packages of cheese and crackers, a bag of vanilla wafers, and my inhaler with an extra refill. MY INHALER!

Rolling over onto my right side, my breathing became excessively labored. Fumbling with the zipper, I pulled the bag closer to me. Jules heard the rustling. Coming to my side, she thought I was becoming delirious. She pushed me over onto my back. I struggled. Being on my back made things even worse. No strength remained to resist. In my most audible voice, a whispered hush, like Darth Vader, I told her that my inhaler was in the backpack. She leaned close to hear me. Wildly my hands searched for the backpack as I repeated my statement. Jules turned and extended her hand, feeling the backpack.

"Oh!" I heard Jules say, as a dim, filtered light cascaded down on us. She grabbed the pack and rustled around. Gasping for air, I summed enough energy to tell her it was in the inside pocket. As her hands searched diligently, I saw her look up, her features lit by the cascading light. She nodded for me to look too.

CHAPTER 3

GREEN, GREEN GRASS OF HOME

As Jules' focus returned to unzipping the inner pocket of the backpack, Daichi let out a victory howl. A hazy light filtered in through the puncture he made. Avery hurriedly worked his way over to Daichi's side holding the grassy part that had folded over, as Daichi ripped through it with the Buck knife. With each subsequent puncture and pull, I could hear the roots being torn apart. Straining my neck to see, shadows extended as the light filtered in. My energy waned. My head dropped back onto the sweater Jules had placed as a pillow.

As the turf was pulled away, Jules helped me into a sitting position, she sat on the side of me so I could lean against her. My inhaler had dropped from my hand as I was sitting up. Frantically I began feeling around. Jules realized that I was looking for my inhaler.

"Relax, I'll find it." She said in a matter-of-fact tone that I knew she would. Within a few moments she held the inhaler up for me to breathe in. Anticipated relief filled my soul as I wrapped my lips around the extended nozzle. With her forefinger and palm steadying it, Jules' thumb pushed up against the tiny aerosol can. A blast of medicated air rushed into my mouth, I breathed as deep as I could. Prompting her with a squeeze to her hand, she repeated the action. Another blast filled my mouth. The first blast now worked opening my bronchial tubes, I visualized the capillaries opening up to receive the medicated mist. The second blast went deeper as the air passages in my lungs opened, which spasmed causing me to cough.

With my breathing on its way to being restored, my body relaxed. Every muscle of my body ached from the tension. Jules pushed the backpack over and encouraged me to lean against it. I scooted down so my shoulders lay on the backpack. Jules then propped the sweater between me and the backpack. Stretching out my legs, I lay there while the others worked at releasing us. Jules left me and went to Avery and Daichi who were now working overhead. Dirt clots fell onto me, the light expanded to fill the grassy capsule. They were slitting the grassy capsule in half. As the top was torn, Avery and Jules pushed on opposite sides. With the last insertion of the knife, they leaned into the walls. Both went tumbling down with the grassy walls to the ground. A burst of laughter cascaded down on me, Daichi had seen both fall simultaneously. As often happens during tense times, contagiously the laughter spread. Avery rose slowly to his feet, chuckling. Jules roared with laughter, rolling onto her back, her body reverberated. She stomped her feet, her face streaming with tears.

This sight made us all laugh even more. Wheezing, I had to finally look away and compose myself. Jules heaved deep breaths in an attempt to contain herself. Each time she looked over at Avery the laughter began again.

"Okay, Okay," Jules repeated, "I have to get up." Her voice was suddenly serious but inflected with muffled giggles as she gradually regained her composure. Avery had risen and walked over to pull Jules up to her feet. Jules brushed dirt and grass from her arms and pant legs and her, okay I have to say it, her jelly butt.

She stated the obvious to the others in a hushed voice.

"We have to get him off this grass. His whole body is full of welts and the inhaler won't work if he keeps breathing in the stuff, he's allergic to." It was awkward to hear her talk as if I wasn't even there.

"Pollen," Avery quipped.

"What?" Daichi and Jules questioned.

"Pollen, it's pollen he is allergic to." Avery answered.

"Pollen, are you sure, isn't that what flowers produce and bees gather?" Daichi asked.

Avery began to interject. Jules stopped him saying in a not so hushed voice, "Really! Really?" She said in a sarcastic tone, then with a serious intonation said, "This is not the time to debate this issue! We need to move him. Now!"

Daichi muttered, "Oh it was fine when you were laughing your butt off." Jules shot him a look to kill.

Avery and Jules lifted me to my feet. Daichi stood watching.

"Daichi! grab the backpack," Jules' voice was filled with agitation.

It was decided that Avery would stay with me since he had the most experience dealing with me, well and my asthma. Jules and Daichi would scout the area to see if there was a way out of here.

"What is up with you calling me Daichi? You think you're my mother? You know only Mom can call me that." His voice grew faint as distance grew between us and them. I couldn't hear Jules' answer, but I chuckled to myself that I have been calling him Daichi here in my journal. I better start calling him Daichi or he will murderize me if he gets hold of this. Dai or Daichi that is what he wants, no insists on being called.

Avery had me sit up so he could get a water for us to share. Silence, an eerie silence, permeated the cavern. Avery looked around, into the nothingness surrounding us. The rustling of my laying back down on the backpack broke his trance. He squatted by me, he held the water bottle as I sipped. Once I got a mouthful I pushed it away, letting the water slowly drain down my throat. Avery took a swallow and twisted the cap back on. Eyes welling with tears, he fought back emotion. Realizing I was watching him he playfully smacked my leg and said,

"What you lookin' at, geekster?" He handed me the bottle after twisting the cap back off. "One more drink for you." He emphasized you. "We need to get those histamines out of your system."

Wow, Avery did pay attention. Tears welled up in my eyes as I realized he cared. Something I would never accuse him of, guys don't do that stuff.

"I am going to be, okay?" Pulling my lips away from the bottle, I half stated, and half asked. Drops of water slid down my chin, following the contours of my neck, before being absorbed by my cotton tee shirt.

Avery issued this assurance, "Sure, dweeb face, Mom will kill me if anything happens to you." As he spoke, he looked past me. Anxiety filled his eyes as he searched through the filtered light in hopes of seeing Jules and Daichi. It was futile. He turned his attention back to me.

"How are you doing? Your breathing still getting better? I remember Mom saying that after about five minutes if you aren't breathing better, it's okay for you to have another puff. You think you need one, or are you getting better?" He bombarded me with too many questions to answer. How was I going to nod or shake my head to all of that? I simply uttered, "More."

I let him take the inhaler from my hand. Placing the nozzle on my lips he squeezed one more medicated blast through my respiratory system. This seemed to push the previous ones further in. My breathing began to be much easier.

Avery had checked his cell phone as the scouting party left. There was no signal to call out, but the clock worked. He checked it again.

"Forty-five minutes," he stated. What had seemed to be an eternity had been forty-five minutes.

Avery struggled to rise from the squatting position beside me.

"See I told ya! You needed to build your lower body instead of always worrying 'bout those pecs." As Avery looked down at me, shaking his head, a smile emerged.

"You are such a dweeb!" The normalcy of this exchange was comforting.

Breathless, Jules and Daichi returned. Jules spoke first.

With heaving breaths, she said, "We found a cave that will serve as a shelter. It is warm and dry. Let's go and get him settled."

"A shelter? I thought you went to find a way out?" I asked with irritation as if they went to get ice cream and forgot the cones.

"We couldn't find a way out, "Jules stammered then added, "Yet, we couldn't find a way out yet."

Solemnly, I nodded, realizing that they wanted out of here as much as I did. It wasn't their fault they couldn't find a way out. Daichi helped me to my feet. I followed Jules to the shelter.

Avery picked up my backpack and flung it over one shoulder. He would regret that in his forties, I could hear my mother's words. My heart sank. Would I ever hear my mother's voice again? I noticed we all had heavy steps as we trudged away from the grassy patch of our home into the dark, dusty unknown. The only light was the strange filtered light from above.

Avery used his cell phone as a flashlight. It was decided that the other two would save their batteries. I remembered that I had a small flashlight on the keychain attached to the backpack, and mother, in her infinite wisdom, had put extra batteries in a separate pouch which I had complained about bulging and not looking cool.

Again, her voice rang, "Well, being cool or being prepared, which would you rather be?"

I was fourteen and apparently underdeveloped as the hormone initiating defiance of all my parents stood for had not come crashing through my system. I didn't fight it. So, I was uncool by proxy. I really wasn't the nerd everyone thought I was, I just didn't have the gumption to argue every minor detail with my mother.

I whispered to Jules about the batteries.

She responded teasingly, "Am I ever glad you are a nerd!" Jules then said to the whole group, "When we get there, we need to figure out what we have that will help us. Puberbs has a flashlight and batteries."

Daichi laughed, "Puberbs, good one, Jules."

The lamp to our roadway was a cell phone, I shook my head at the irony of the whole or should I say hole situation. I was cracking myself up. I began to tell the others but realized the humor would be lost in translation. I crawled out of my head and rejoined the reality of the situation around me. Dust particles in the air added density which filtered the light even more. Visibility was about six feet, six feet into dark nothingness. As the cavern widened and narrowed, the wall of cold stone weaved within our reach accordingly.

Time was magnified by darkness void of landmarks. We reached a tunnel that led to the cave. The floor was hard rock. "Too bad we can't have the gr...." Daichi began to say, Avery and Jules, both interrupted him. Avery spoke over Jules, "Okay, we need to see what we have to work with regarding food, tools and other survival stuff." He hefted the backpack off his shoulder. "Before I open this, what other stuff do we have?"

"I'll start." It was Daichi. He began emptying his pockets. "I have a lighter."

"A lighter?" Jules' tone was filled with accusation, accusation as only a sister can project. "A lighter? Really. Really?" Demanding a response.

"Smoker chicks ask for a light and I do. That way I avoid the "do you smoke drama." Daichi defended.

"Really, really? You're serious? What if they ask for a cigarette? Do you carry them too?!" According to my assessment of the situation she was reacting a bit harshly. Here we were trapped in the center of the earth and Jules was concerned about what ifs.

Daichi answered, "No! If they ask for a cigarette, I say I am out. No lie, I was never in." He laughed. Jules realized the intensity of her inquisition was off balance. With some reluctance she laughed too.

"Whatever, it is a good thing he has one," Avery interjected.

Daichi went on to share that he had, of course, his Buck knife and lighter. Three paper clips, a pack of gum, a few screws, and a pacifier.

"A pacifier?" All of us asked in unison. Defensively, he explained. He had taken baby Kiera, Jules and his niece to the park yesterday. He grabbed the same jeans this morning he had worn the night before.

In unison again, we all said, "They are hatin' you right now!"

Then it occurred to us that this pacifier may lead them to start looking for us. That and the gaping-hole in our backyard.

A few coins and that concluded Daichi's contributions. Jules was next. She pulled a small purse and a bottle of water from the pouch of her hoodie. Besides feminine unmentionables, at least unmentionable by this fourteen-year-old boy, she had two safety pins, a chocolate bar, half a roll of Sweet Tarts, an emery board, a tiny sewing kit, a pair and a half of earrings, her driver's license and her mother's ATM card.

"Mom's ATM card?" Daichi asked. We all looked at her in anticipation for an answer.

"She sent me to the store to get some Redbox movies last night and some snacks!" Jules responded defensively, adding "Well, between this and the pacifier, I bet they are scouring the town looking for us!"

Her voice was jovial but edged with nervousness.

Avery was next. Pulling his pockets inside out he scooped out a few sunflower seeds and thirty-five cents from one. From the other pocket came a movie ticket stub, a pair of nail clippers, an eraser and twenty-three dollars in mixed bills and a rubber band. Jules picked up the ticket stub. It was from *Eat, Pray, Love* the first movie and the last chick flick they had gone to. Her eyes got all melty as she sighed. Reaching over, she hugged

Avery. For him this was a bittersweet moment. It would have been really sweet had they been alone, and he could have garnished the rewards of her appreciative affection freely. Instead, self-restraint prevailed since it was not only in front of guys but in front of us, their brothers. The two males whose sole duty regarding Jules and Avery as a couple was to make them feel awkwardly aware of their emotions.

Daichi started. In a high pitched, feminine tone, "Oh, Avery, you are just sooo sentimental. How long did it take you to wipe the lipstick off your lips from your first kiss? Or do you still have the tissue you used to wipe it off with?" He turned to Jules, "Oh Romeo, oh Romeo!"

I was wheezing with laughter. Daichi turned to me for recognition and solidarity. I nodded in approval. Jules retorted, "You two are such losers. Immature, no wonder you don't have a girlfriend, Daichi."

"I can't decide which one I want," he defended and looked again to me for approval.

Nodding, I said, "Yeah!" which came out quite deep and throaty due to my asthmatic condition. I sounded kinda cool. Though the medicated postnasal drip rolling down my throat might cancel out the coolness.

Avery firmly brought us back to the moment. Harshly he said, "Pubes, what about you? I mean besides the backpack."

Holding to true pubescent form, I pulled my pockets inside out: seven dollars and fifty-two cents, a couple of screws, a rubber band, a marble, a sticky with a phone number and that was it. The backpack was my big-ticket item. The contents had already been discussed. We decided to open a bottle of water to share, adding one of the packets of vitamin flavoring to it. We split two granola bars between us.

As we rationed the food a sense of desperation hung over us. Each bite was taken with silent care. None of us had been in a situation where food was truly scarce. Oh, we had each looked in the fridge and cabinets brimming with consumables and hollered to our mothers, "There is nothing here to eat!" Which translated from teenage lingo means, "There is no quick fix junk food brimming with MSG and preservatives to over stimulate and dull desire for real, whole foods!"

The thought of no food was sobering. I looked at each of the others as they thoughtfully chewed each morsel. Jules looked up. Her eyes met mine. They were filled with anxiety; she bravely curled her lips in a halfhearted attempt to smile. I turned away; afraid she would see the fear welling up within me.

"My, well, Daichi's and my great grandparents were peasant farmers in Japan. Naitu told of going without food for days, she says that the third day your stomach stops nagging you." Jules offered as comfort.

We were doomed! I remembered studying the core of the earth. There was no sunlight except the filtered light from the hole created when the ground collapsed around us. Surrounding us was hard rock. The layers lined the walls of the cavern, creating a marbleized relief. Nothing could grow down here. I stood up and walked over to the wall, which radiated with cool dampness.

We were trapped! Anxiety caused my heart rate to increase. I could feel it thumping in my chest. I closed my eyes, fighting to hold back the frustration fueled tears. I pinched them away with my thumb and forefinger. Panic would serve no purpose. I needed to regain composure. Leaning my head against the cold wall of rock, I had to face the others. I looked over. Daichi was carefully controlling his emotions. His breathing was labored, and he refused to make eye contact with me.

If we were to get through this, we needed to talk. We needed to come up with a strategy. We needed to focus intensely on a solution. We faced an overwhelming challenge. We needed to pray to a God we rarely acknowledged. The means of which we entered this abyss was certainly not a means in which we could exit.

Looking at the three of them, Avery sat cross legged, Jules and Daichi squatted. Their sturdy legs dispersed their body weight. Jules appeared mesmerized. I cleared my voice to speak, only to be interrupted gratefully, by Avery. He sat up straight and motioned me to come closer. I complied.

In a calm, clear voice Avery spoke. "We are in...." From the passageway we followed to this point, a clamoring noise erupted. Jules, hunching now closer to the ground, looked up. Daichi sprang to his feet as Avery struggled to unwrap his legs and finally stand. I reached down urging Jules up. Instinctively we fled to the shadows of the cavern, along the wall. Daichi had grabbed the backpack, but much of the contents lay spilled on the cavern floor along with my seven dollars and other contents from my pockets.

The clamoring subsided. I could hear hushed voices speaking as deliberate footsteps drew near. The others acknowledged the voices with exaggerated facial expressions. We exchanged wide-eyed looks. Breathing slowly and deliberately, I knew we all shared the mixed emotions of terror and rejoicing. We were not alone and that of course could either be wonderful or devastating, depending on the disposition of those approaching.

A torch filled the cavern with light. The source also illuminated the creature that was holding it. The position of the light darkened the shadowed area where we hid. I could determine that the creature holding the light was quite corpulent. Lacking definitive features, tiny legs projected to the ground and a spindly arm held the torch. The creature turned back, communicating with those following. The voice was masculine, and I could distinguish an Irish accent. An Irish accent? I kept on with my assessment. The skin of the creature was rough and gritty brown, studded with white eruptions, some of which had tiny eyes. These eruptions moved, seeming to scan the area like tiny lenses of video cameras. I looked over at the other three. They stared in wide eyed amazement. Avery and I made eye contact. Without words we shared our stunned dismay.

The followers murmured amongst themselves. They appeared to be assessing the walls of the cavern. We pushed ourselves as flat as we could. One spoke. The rest hushed each other. The One spoke, "What du ya see, thar?" The one holding the torch came to the center of the cave and pushed the torch toward the walls. "Nuthin. Let's go, dis is eerie. We need to go and see where the light is coming frum. Come on, we gotta see what is thar, thar is nothing here." The Second one insisted.

Of course! The sink hole would be a major catastrophe to anyone dwelling down here. If it was a natural phenomenon then they too had been caught by surprise. It seemed apparent that they had not caused it and if they had it had been quite accidental. Though I could not make out exactly what was being said, the group was in a panic. The way they scurried around kind of reminded me of the Ewoks from Star Wars. What sounded like gibberish to me, flowed from them in spurts. My attention went back to the Torch Holder. Turning back toward the spot we had been sitting, he noticed the items spilled out on the floor. A water bottle, some sunflower seeds, and my inhaler. He walked over and peered down at the items. His rotund body did not bend. He swiveled to face the others. Motioning to the group leader to come. Laboriously bending over, his arm extended farther than I had anticipated. He picked up the water bottle and the inhaler in his oversized hand. A command was directed from the group. He turned sweeping the area again with light. This time slowly. Everyone in the cave, them and us were trembling. We had all turned our heads, cheeks pressing against the wall as if we could become one with it. As we pressed as close as we could, the light fell, pushing back our cover of darkness. We were exposed!

CHAPTER 4

ALL EYES UPON US

The creatures' eyes followed the light directly to Jules. They each let out a scream and the torch fell to the ground followed by the inhaler and the water bottle. The water bottle rolled under the one that had been holding the torch. With a thud it landed. Its rotund shape rendered him helpless. Flailing around in his attempts to right himself, only to spin himself into a wobble.

All eyes turned to the spectacle. We looked over to the group of creatures who had emerged out of the tunnel and into the mouth of the cave. When I say all eyes, I mean all kinds of eyes! Along with the two eyes on the area that I determined to be their face. Tiny eyes protruded from all over their bodies. The flickering of the light made it hard to see, but I made out that their brown skin was pitted with dirt, it had a sort of burlap texture. Giant potatoes! I guess their kids would be Tater Tots, I cracked myself up!

Anyway, a smaller red skinned one grabbed the torch from the ground. The lack of urgency was grounded in the fact that there was nothing combustible around, just dirt. Suddenly there was a POP! A searing hiss sounded through the cavern. We covered our ears. The creatures all raised their tiny arms upward to cover tubes that appeared to tunnel into their flesh above their arm sockets. The intensity of the whistling was outrageous. The decibels reverberated against our eardrums painfully. The creatures emitted a high-pitched sound almost matching in decibels to the one that continued to assault our eardrums.

I looked down at the source of the sound. At that moment my inhaler turned into a projectile, shooting up and to the right, ricocheting off that wall then the wall on the left of us. The velocity being reduced only slightly with each point of impact. We all strained to keep track of the object. Our necks spun our heads following the projectile. The Potato People's cabled eyes extended and retracted as they followed the track of the now slowing projectile.

Then what happened was bizarre. Cables of two of the Potato People's eyes had gotten wrapped around each other. As they struggled to get free from one another, they toppled to the floor. My inhaler! The reality had only now sunk in. I filled with panic. No, I could not panic, it could lead to another asthma attack. I inhaled several deep breaths.in and out, to calm myself. As I did, the capsule, exhausted of inertia, spinning slowly to a stop at my feet with all eyes on it. Then as a whole the group turned all their eyes on us and then back to the inhaler. They were agitated and rightly, so the inhaler scared the bee doggies out of all of us.

Attention was then given to their fallen comrades. Our eyes also settled on the two struggling on the ground, each letting out a flourish of inconceivable sounds. One of the others attempted to reach the intertwined eye cables to untangle them. Panic set in as the two on the ground wrestled and made the job harder for the one trying to help. The Torch Holder and one other stood in a ready position focusing most of their eyes on us. The rest turned their attention to the fallen Potatoes. The crowd scurried awkwardly and spoke to one another in excited tones.

Already imprisoned in the center of the Earth, now we were faced with quite a dilemma. The Potatoes were little threat, I knew we could outrun them, running to where, I have no idea. Watching them struggle with a situation that we could easily solve gave me the courage to step forward. Clearing my throat, I extended my hands out to show I held no weapons or intention of harm. I chuckled to myself, no potato peelers here, no paring knives, okay I'll stop.

Glancing back to the faces of the humanoids I traveled with their eyes filled with fear and anxiety. Avery reached out to stop me. I shrugged him away as I turned my attention back to the two struggling on the floor, they too had eyes filled with astonishment and anxiety. This made me realize that I too shared the state of those around me. I began to wonder what possessed me to be so bold. Oh, yeah, nothing to lose.

I heard a moment of intense discussion from both sides. Then I heard Daichi's feet scuffle as Jules and Avery pushed him forward to join me. I nudged Daichi with my shoulder and looked intently at my outstretched arms. He followed my lead. We looked into the primary eyes of the one guarding the group. Gesturing toward the fallen two with my outstretched arms, I cautiously squatted down and made gestures showing that I had the flexibility to bend and the dexterity in my fingers to unravel the cables.

The Guardian shouted to the others that we wanted to help, pointing over to Daichi and I. After a bit of discussion, the group gathered around the two, the Guardian spoke to us. "Comm' on ova ear."

Grateful that they understood, we gingerly crossed the distance between the fallen Potatoes and us. I bent over to assess the situation. Daichi stood dividing his attention between me and those gathered around. The Guardian hollered across the cavern to Avery and Jules, "You two, coom'on ova ear." Soon Avery and Jules were watching as I lifted the entwined cables into my hand to examine. It felt like calamari. I stood up as Avery took the Potato person's hands in his, and Daichi lifted from behind, righting the Potato onto its oversized feet. We repeated the process for the second Potato.

As they stood regaining their senses, I noticed, at the same time the Torch Holder did, that one of the roots of the recently entwined cables was oozing a white starchy liquid. The Torch Holder gasped in horror and began speaking in what sounded like Gaelic.

My sixth-grade class had studied Ireland last year in depth since it was the ancestral home of my teacher Mr. Korbarlaczk. When Geena Kinsky said in a quite accusing tone that he was not Irish since his last name was Polish. Mr. Korbarlaczk responded in a quite defensive tone that he was Irish from his mother's side of the family. Geena then made the observation that he was not Irish, but half Irish. Mr. Korbarlaczk turned bright red and continued with his story, ignoring Geena's further attempts to comment on his genealogy. I was shaken from my mental excursion by emphatic gesturing and the pleas for me to "peek up the durt" by the Torch Holder. As I stood there confused, the Torch Holder stopped with the pleas and authoritatively commanded, without the thick brogue of the Guardian, "Pick up the dirt!"

Hurriedly, I bent down and grabbed a handful of the silty dirt. I was then instructed to gather some of the oozing liquid and form a paste with it. At first, I resisted, who knew what pathogens might be in the ooze. The Torch Holder's intense gaze glassing over into a glare motivated me. So much for not being intimidated by the Potatoes. I had started this, so I had to finish it. Reluctantly I captured some of the oozing liquid in the palm of the hand holding the dirt. I mixed with my free hand until a paste was formed.

The next step was to pack the muddy starch salve around the base of the oozing cable. The observing Potatoes joined the wounded one with thanking me, well, me and Daichi. A thick white hand, that looked as if it were gloved, patted me not so gently on the back. It was followed by several more. As my back began to throb from the appreciation, I side stepped my way out of their reach. I turned and bowed in acknowledgement of the appreciation as I had seen Jules and Daichi do before and after speaking with their grandparents.

The rest of the Potatoes that had been conferencing stopped when they heard the Torch Holder command me to pick up the dirt. I looked over to Jules, Bird, and Daichi. Oh, Avery, birds live in an aviary, so I call Avery, Bird, wow I don't know where that came from. A mental shift, I guess. The Potatoes had looks of disbelief and dismay as they assessed us. Would we be heroes or captives? Our fate hung in the balance. I took a few steps back and joined the three of them, right between Bird and Jules. A coveted spot that if we were not facing mortal danger would have been met with firm and effective resistance and probably a cuff from Bird.

The two rescued Potatoes stood aside and sent hopeful glances to us. The rest gathered and were entrenched in debate, yes, debate regarding our fate. All the while they stood blocking the entrance, or now the exit, of the cave. The Leader was suspicious of us. With his rich Irish accent, we were unable to decipher details, but it was obvious it had a vehement opinion, and it was not in our favor. Its cable eyes had been drawn away from us as he argued his point. One by one the cables pulled eyes into alignment with us, without him turning around. Seeing that their conversation had our attention, he began speaking Gaelic. The others strained hard to hear the Leader's whispered tone.

Watching the response of the others it was obvious that not all of them were fluent in Gaelic. Some were whispering interpretations to others. Some were obviously bored with the whole situation. The Two wounded ones had edged their way over to us, hidden to the group by a jutting of the wall. The deep shadows made this the perfect place for them to hide. We had watched them with our peripheral vision, trying hard not to alert the group still arguing, yes, the debate had turned into an argument exponentiated in ferocity by the lack of communal participation. It was the largest and crustiest Peeps that continued. The smaller and smoother textured were unable to keep up with the ancient tongue.

"PSSST," Jules looked over her shoulder. A finger emerged from the shadows motioning for her to come closer. We all caught on and spaced ourselves out, leaning against the wall, making it look like we were all resting. Jules squatted, leaning her forearms on her thighs. She turned towards me.

"When I talk, nod your head and look like you're talking to me." Jules said.

Wow, I thought, she is so flippin' smart, covert, like a spy smart. I felt awesome being a key player in the plot. I focused on Jules as if we were having a conversation. The debate across the way had some of the Potatoes boiling mad. I couldn't resist that one. Okay, back with Jules.

I heard a muffled voice speak from the shadows. Jules would repeat what was said to her in a voice just loud enough for us to make out. I kept facing her. Bird, oh, Avery and Daichi had moved closer to us. We were clustered in the nook created by the jutting wall. The story took a while to relay. Just as the last words were said and the Two made it back to their original spot the group disbanded. There was confusion as they shuffled into ranks. The Two took their place among their peers.

The Leader, accompanied by a smaller Potato, made their way over to us. The Leader spoke in his rich Irish brogue. The Small One translated to us. The Leader wanted us to come willingly with them back to their community. The Potatoes were grateful for our assistance untangling the two. It would have meant certain death for them if we had not intervened. This said, the Small One translated that the Leader had many dealings with humans. None of which were pleasant. As the small one translated the Leader muttered the Machiavellian phrase, "Keep your friends close and your enemies closer, I know their tactics."

Avery and I looked at one another and agreed that he thought we were part of some kind of sinister plot. Tears welled up in my eyes. Home, I just want to be at home complaining about lima beans and liver. The Small One looked over at the Leader wanting to know if he wanted his last statement interpreted.

The Leader waved his hand dismissing the comment but then said, "Before decisions of their fate could be discussed we need to learn who sent them and the details of their mission." Which the Small One hesitantly interpreted.

"Whaa, what mission?" I stammered. "Oh goodness sakes" (remember my mom may read this) I said to the others, "they think we are spies; they think we have a mission; they think...." Jules smacked me on the arm. "Get a hold of yourself!"

Jules stepped up to listen to the interpreter, "We will not treat you as hostiles unless you become hostile. The communication will continue in the comforts of our community. You are showing signs of dehydration. Human's lips grow dry and yours are all cracking, we must get you water." With that we were herded through to the tunnel that had led us to the cave.

The Two that were untangled were assigned to escort us as we walked. They slowed our pace and consoled us as we walked. Not all the counsel feels as this Leader does. The Two gave us a rundown of the Potahs' history. It seems that the Irish potato famine was not as it seemed. I had been told in social studies that there had been a scarcity of food in Ireland except for potatoes. According to the legends of the Potahs, as they called themselves, there was plenty of food, but it was loaded into wagons and tossed into the sea. This was so people would only consume potatoes to rid Ireland of potatoes and then the rest of the world. The result was horrendous. Potatoes had their skins peeled off, they were diced, sliced, julienned, boiled, mashed, roasted, fried, smothered in molten cheese, and baked. This created terror within the Potah community which was soon reduced to a mere twenty-five potatoes.

The Leader was just a spud when all of this was happening but before due time, he had to take on the thick skin of a Russet and become a renegade. There were five others who were the same. The six of them did all they could to rescue their kin from such despicable fates but to no avail. The humans were too formidable of an adversary having an unending supply of weapons of destruction. Stories were told of whole burlap bags of Potahs found in cellars, blackened with rot and maggot infested. The carnage was beyond horrific. Families separated, Tater Tots were thrown into hot grease and served with eggs and bacon to the aristocrats, who had a penchant for the tender young starch of the unformed potato. The Two shivered as they related the stories, to myself I trembled because it never occurred to me that potatoes were well, Potahs. I was guilty of these crimes. My heartbeat wildly recounting the stories, what if they found out? We would definitely lose our status as willing guests. I shook the thought from my mind. Maybe they weren't aware of the eating habits of contemporary humans.

Back to the story. Of the six the Leader and another escaped the boiling oil vat. This left only twenty-three, no twenty-two, sorry bad math skills, Potahs. These went underground, literally. They created the illusion of gestating potatoes. Before entering the ground, each performed a feat of courage never matched. They ripped out three of their cables, a risky act tantamount to a human cutting off an appendage. Cutting a cable can lead to starch infection permeating their system or worse, for them to ooze to death. Bravely they risked it all to save their species. Ten of the Potahs ripped their own cables out. Twelve had to have the others do it for them. Of the twenty-two, eleven succumbed to starch infection and slowly decayed in the dirt, a treacherous fate. Three oozed to death. A death whose details are not even spoken of, it was so horrific.

The other eight had to thicken their skins even more to survive. They burrowed further than a Potah had ever gone before. Leaving their detached cables as a decoy to humans. The humans would pour kerosine over the soil around the exposed cables and light them on fire, a technique used instead of ripping the gestating Potah from the ground, risking leaving a root behind that may generate more potatoes. Far below the fiery surface the Potahs would be burrowing to safety, soft dirt filling the holes as they burrowed, sealing any clues as to where they had gone.

Their burrowing came to an abrupt halt as they passed through the ceiling of the catacomb of caverns, landing on the hard cold ground of a tunnel nearby where we had been deposited. They had initially panicked since Potahs must have soft, enriched soil to survive. As they assessed their situation, each fearful to vocalize their apprehension, piles of dirt came cascading through the holes they had burrowed. Though the burrow had a sealed topside, the loose dirt beyond that seal had followed them down, resulting in eight huge piles of soil pleasantly engulfing them. Shouts of glee echoed, twisting through the catacombs. According to Potah legend, in the stillness of the night the echoes can still be heard traveling through the caverns. Parent Potahs tell of this happy ending as bedtime stories, leaving out the gruesome details of the revolution. As they came of age, they would have a catechism regarding their history and the faith it represents.

Three of the Potahs had been sealed beneath the piles. Though a disaster to a human, Potahs natural habitat was to be encased in soil. The others dove in to join their comrades. Our Two escorts spoke of a celebration secured by legend of tufts of dirt being flung into the air. Laughter rose. The Potahs took the generous deposit of soil as a sign of good tidings from the Great Norkotah.

The Two had to abruptly end their conversation with us as a group of others came to relieve them. I reflected as we walked. Looking back at Daichi and forward to Jules and Avery, I presumed they were thinking the same thing I was. Avery's eyes gave him away, he looked at me and without words conveyed to me his apprehension at reaching the destination. This got me thinking. What would we find? Would we be honored or feared? Though my legs were aching from the distance covered I wanted the journey to continue as not to face the destination. Swallowing hard, hoping to keep my fear from being evident. I missed my mom and dad. They had to be looking for us. Yes, of course they are looking for us, it would take time to develop a strategy and gather the people and equipment necessary to rescue us. When all this was formulated in my mind, I wished we could have stayed where we landed. My feet kept moving.

A golden light filled the tunnel. The Potahs all stopped. We followed suit. They chanted something in Gaelic then bowed, as well as they could, toward the golden glow. My attention went back and forth to the Potahs and the beautiful golden light. The rest of the journey was in complete silence as we became engulfed in the light. We turned a final corner and could see the source of the golden glow. Two giant arches were set as the gateway to the Potahs' land. A drawbridge extended out, as a golden pathway. The Wizard of Oz's song about the yellow brick road skipped around in my head as we continued through the golden arches, the golden arches? Yes, they looked like magnificent arches I had seen around town. My mind conjured up a Big Mac and fries so real I could smell them. How I longed for my normal life, I hoped that this would all be a dream, yes of course, a dream and I would wake up in my grandfather's spare room with quilted comforters covering me. I pinched myself hoping to jar myself awake, Nothing, I was still here.

The line filed through the arch as others used the second arch as an egress. Wide eyed I looked around. The walls of the cavern were lined with rows of boxes, like the garden boxes at Aunt Jody's where she grew cabbage and lettuce. These were both small and large. Some held many sections, others just one. There was a giant machine wiggling to and fro sifting dirt that was dumped into it. The sifted dirt was put into boxes on a conveyor belt taking the refined soil up to the boxes set into the cavern wall. This was only dropped on Potahs present in their boxes. It showered down on them and they smeared it around onto themselves like I did soap when I take a shower. The rich soil was then patted down around the Potahs as they settled in.

There was so much going on. To the right I could see Potahs covered in netting working behind a glass wall, the closest thing I can compare it to would be a laboratory. With thick glasses attached to the cable eyes, tiny starch like things were examined and evidently accepted or rejected. An image reflecting from the glass sent my head whirling around. Behind me was a Ferris wheel type object that lifted the Potahs to various staggered ledges. There was one small Potah running the simple mechanism at the bottom. The Potahs would disembark at a ledge that sported colored flags that matched the color of the hard hat the Potah wore. Highly polished hard hats refracted the light glowing from the arches. Tools were carried in boxes. It reminded me of Weebles. I had a Ferris Wheel Weeble set as a kid, well it had been my mom's friend's neighbor's...it had been given to me. That's what they looked like as they wobbled toward the tunnels just wide enough that two could pass going in and out.

Two disappeared down one tunnel and came out on the next ledge carrying two buckets full of dark soil. The Ferris wheel was loaded with the buckets and the Potah was dropped back off on the ledge. I watched this be repeated on each of the ledges. Potahs would go in one tunnel and come out on the next level. This was a very curious thing to watch. The system seemed to go flawlessly. I was jarred back to my immediate surroundings as the Potahs resumed the march. We were taken through a less ominous set of arches into a courtyard. The Two stayed with us. The rest, except the Leader and another seemingly subordinate, continued their march down several pathways in groups of four or eight.

I looked around, while they continued to carry out their tasks, a few cable eyes of each studied us with curiosity. Recalling the history of the Potahs I felt shame in the pit of my stomach. I had no idea that potatoes were such complex and intelligent creatures. The potatoes that we eat the two told me were mutant hybrids whose personality and intellect have been muted over the generations that separated the Potahs from them.

I asked how they knew so much about the Topside, as they called it. The two responded in unison, "If we told you we would have to kill you." There was an inkling of play in their voice, but I believed they meant it. As all these thoughts churned within my mind, my feet had brought us through a great passageway, gargantuan doors made of stone opened to each side of the passage. Two Potahs stood on each side of the entrance. My gaze extended, taking in the beauty surrounding us. As my eyes leveled to the front, I gasped in horror at what I saw. Jules squeezed Avery's arm and buried her face in his chest. Daichi turned away to keep this vision from being etched into his memory.

CHAPTER 5

COURT SIDE SEATS

It was a mural depicting the horrors of the Potato Famine. In the center the Great Norkotah sat, on a celestial plot of the most refined soil. His scepter pointed down toward the carnage below. Horrific potato hunts vanquished the Potahs from their land, their soil, their homes. The mural was aged, and the paint was peeling. Still, we were able to see the frying, baking, boiling and other heinous acts that could not even be mentioned, all at the hands of humankind. As my eyes took in the carnage, I looked upon another wall which showed the vindication of those lost by the hand of Norkotah. Golden arches rose up to the throne in which he sat with his scepter pointed up toward the topside of the Earth. Potah warriors avenging the blood of their ancestors.

Avenging them with the blood of humanity. I gulped. Jules looked at me and conveyed a strength I needed to see. We would have to prove trustworthy. We had to prove our innocence. They had to know we were just kids, goofy harmless kids. Hopefully they have studied our culture enough to know the only thing we are interested in is Xbox.

We were urged in through the entrance and past the murals. We were taken into a theater like auditorium with rows upon rows rising in tiers away from the stage. On the stage were four sets of two Potahs standing stately, their cable eyes scanning. We were led up the side stairs and along a golden carpet and I mean literally golden carpet. As we walked two Potahs followed us sweeping up any trace of debris. A necessity when the whole population dropped clumps of dirt as they walked. One of the Two told me that they recycle the dirt. Ah, environmentalist Potahs.

We turned right, away from the tiers of chairs. The carpet continued, did I tell you it was literally golden, oh yea, never mind. Doors were set into the back wall of the stage, centered. The Potahs are a very symmetrical species. With their disdain for humans, I am certainly not going to call them people. As we approached the doors two of the Potahs reached out and pulled them open, holding them until we passed through. The group guarding us diminished. Six were left escorting us. The Leader and the Small One, The Two stood on each side of us as the Leader took his place among the gathered Council. The Small One stood behind him as did others behind each member.

Another two stood behind us. The council member sitting in the center of the semi-circle spoke. The voice was noticeably feminine. A crown hovered above her, moving as she did. "Who do I have before me?" She rose out of her soil box. Two small Potahs rose with her, draping a shimmering burlap cape around her. We would learn that the council members wore burlap in memory of those who gave their lives during the persecution of the Potato Famine.

One of the Two began to speak. "Silence" her tone was firm but not condemning, "These can communicate for themselves. Please, the, well, adolescents. Neither boys or girls nor men and women." She spoke in a smug tone. "So, first the female. Tell me your name."

"Jules...my name is...Juliana Xi." Jules said nervously.

"Japanese surname and Anglo first name. That is an odd combination. No middle name?" The Crowned One commented.

"Cuifen, Juliana Cuifen Xi." Jules stated more firmly than before.

"Emerald fragrance, a beautiful sentiment. Are you born in May? The birthstone for May is emerald according to custom." Her voice was soft and lilting.

"Yes, I was born in May." Jules said with relief.

"Now you, the one next to our emerald fragrance." She was talking to Avery.

"Avery Carlton Durbin" Avery said this so quickly I was surprised she understood him.

"Oh, goodness we have both a middle name and first name that are of German origin. Let's see Avery, courageous and Carlton, Carl's town." She seemed amused. Durbin? Irish? Her tone grew icy. Avery shuddered. Yet, the female Potah continued assessing the rest of us.

"Ah, and you, the one entering puberty." She turned her attention to me. Cable eyes peering around the cape.

"Joshie, I mean Joshua Christopher Durbin" I said with all the confidence I could muster.

"Are you nervous Joshie? No need to be. Not all in the Council share the archaic beliefs of some. Now, let me think. Am I to suppose you are Avery's brother?" She inquired.

I nodded. She continued. "Joshua, Jehovah saves and Christopher, Christ bearer. Honoring both the Hebrew and Greek origins."

"And, last and most certainly not least. May I have your full name." She motioned toward Daichi with an outstretched hand.

"Daichi Gustav Xi." Daichi spoke in his deepest baritone voice.

"The brother of our emerald fragrance?" She stated rhetorically.

"Japanese first name, a large land or kingdom." She Continued

"And Gustav, Scandinavian for the staff of the gods. My, your names indicate vast diversity." She took a deep breath. "This would tell me you are of the pluralistic culture of the United States and of course the location of your entrance into our realm puts you in the Mojave Desert." She smiled, quite pleased with herself. I have to pass the title of Google master to her.

"Excuse me," I asked politely, "May we know your name, err, what to call you?"

"Beathag (BEH ak). I am known only as Beathag." Her voice sounded distant. Yes, Beathag, no middle or last name." She seemed to realize she had drifted mentally. "Ah, yes, yes, all call me Beathag and so must you." Her tone was welcoming yet firm.

I started to ask, "Why?" Avery reached behind me and thumped me on the back of the head, "Ow, why dya." Another thump. I looked over at him. He gestured for me to keep quiet.

"What is it you want to ask?" Beathag faced me but her cable eyes shifted toward Avery. He put his face down in embarrassment. "Please, go on," her attention was completely on me.

"I, I, well, I wondered what your name means. It must be special since you have only one." I answered and asked her in the same sentence. Secretly stoked that Avery got busted.

"That is a fine question." Her voice rose so that all could hear clearly, but it was directed at Avery. "I am the Offspring of Life, the conduit between my people and the Great Norkotah, where Life originates." Though she answered my question, she went on. After all, she had a captive audience. Cracking myself up!

"I have no terrestrial lineage. The Great Norkotah willed me down to a terrestrial existence when the Potahs took refuge in the Subterrain. My wisdom is to be offered to the Council to deliberate when faced with perplexing decisions." She stopped abruptly as her attention was captured by murmurings of the Leader. "Donnchadh (DO nu chu) have you something to say?" Her tone chastised him. "You are a warrior, and our philosophies will never align. Now, your comment?"

"Begging mercy Beathag. I spoke no ill will toward you. My tongue is silenced." His eyes were downcast when speaking to Beathag.

"Donnchadh, the Brown Warrior, the domestic front is a hard place for a warrior to be." Her attention was toward us, then she turned her cable eyes to him, "A fine warrior, anointed by Beathan (BEH un) my twin brother, whose realm is the mid heavens where battlefield commissions are issued. A fine choice in Donnchadh." Donnchadh sat up straight in his terra firm box. His pride was diplomatically restored.

"Young ones," Her attention was toward us again, "we will perform a purification ceremony to accept you as guests of our extended clan." She noticed us shift uneasily, "Nothing to be afraid of, you would call this a bath and then a rinsing shower followed by a sensory soothing sage session." We all breathed a bit more easily, especially once we found out the sage session was simply having sage incense in the room as we bathed. This was to neutralize any negative energy that may have been produced during our ordeal.

As we were taken away Beathag turned to the Council. There was heated discussion regarding our treatment. I overheard Beathag respond, "I doubt the CIA would send ill equipped teenagers on a reconnaissance mission. For your peace of mind their clothing and belongings will be confiscated and taken to our labs for thorough examination." She spoke with the authority of her position. "Donnachadh, I will trust you with taking care of getting their things to the lab." She stood with cable eyes scanning the members of the Council, "We will follow established protocol in questioning our guests." This protocol the Two shared with us was those questions to be asked needed the approval of the majority of the Council. The tone would be neutral, and our rights would be respected in accord to the Geneva Convention which was the code of humanitarian treatment for prisoners. This part I didn't like. Were we really prisoners? This was the first time that reality fully sunk in, we could not leave if we wanted, and if we could, where would we go? I began to panic as we were led into the bathing area. The sage filled air almost immediately relaxed me, and Avery's reassurance that everything would be fine since we obviously were not CIA or any other kind of spies.

The shower looked conventional. The polished stone floor was encased in a texturized sealant that kept us from slipping. Jules took her shower first. We waited in, with all respect, the sauna. I guess this was some part of a cleansing ritual for the Potahs. I decided to quit thinking and just relax as much as possible.

I was next after Jules. Of course, we let her go first because that is what guys do. Then fortunately for me we decided to go by age in an ascending order. So I was second. The shower felt so good. Dirt filled water ran off me and down the drain. The last time I was this dirty was my last Desert race. My mind wandered back to that race. Forty miles on a dirt bike through a desert course. Brutally, I won my division. Yep, first place, I felt pride well up within me. A familiar banging on the shower room door followed by an irritated, "Hurry up, geek face!" Brought normalcy with it that made me smile and take my time finishing up. When I got out of the shower, finally, I wrapped myself in a plush white bath sheet. These Potah's have class I thought as the banging began again. "I am coming, zit face!" I hollered at him.

As I waited, a smaller red skinned Potah brought me everything I needed to get ready, clothes, a toothbrush, toothpaste, even floss. I turned to Daichi who had come out of the sauna dripping wet with steam rolling off his skin. I handed him a towel to wrap around him. "Where do you think they got all this stuff?"

"Wow, yea, that's a good question," the Neanderthal responded.

As I was pulling up my pants there was a knock on the outer door. "Can I come in?" It was Jules.

"Hold on just a sec," I said as I buttoned and zipped my jeans. I guess they were now mine. "Okay now you can come in, Jules!"

She sat on a bench across from Daichi. She was dressed in skinny jeans and a tee shirt, her hair was in two short braids. "Ah, I feel so much better." She said with a sigh.

"Hurry up, Avery," It was Daichi's turn to bang on the door. Turing to Jules and I, "Can you believe that? Avery went before me because I am eight days older than him." Daichi lamented as he sat back down on the bench facing Jules.

The water turned off. Jules yelled to Avery, "I am out here so keep your towel on!"

As Avery came out of the shower room, Daichi went in. Since the sauna was turned off and had frosted glass Avery opted to change in there so Jules wouldn't have to leave. Jules and I spent time admiring our clothes, amazed that everything fit even our shoes. Jules made a good point, they had our clothes to see the sizes, but that still did not explain where the clothes came from. It did not make sense that the Potahs would have random clothes around for unexpected humanoid guests.

Avery joined us in his new clothes. He and Jules had Earthlings Unite brand tee shirts and shoes. The brand wasn't even in stores yet and could only be ordered online. Everything that has happened since we were sucked to the center of the Earth began revolving in my mind. My asthma attacks. Meeting the Potahs. Being considered guests by some Potahs and prisoners by others. My mom, I missed my mom and dad. I imagined Jules and Daichi's mom looking for her credit card and Jay frantically looking for the pacifier. Of course, they would be looking for us, I mean the house falling into the first sinkhole. They would be searching for us. Even if it looked like we were....I couldn't finish the thought. Tears welled in my eyes. What if no one was looking, what if they presumed the worst? No, mom and dad, Jay, and the rest they would look for us. They had to be able to follow us through the sinkhole. Of course, they can and they would be coming to get us soon. What I didn't know was that the dirt that imploded after us was over a mile thick. We had traveled over three thousand miles beneath the Earth. We were as close as anyone can get and survive to the Earth's molten core. I now understand the saying that ignorance is bliss.

Once Daichi got dressed we were taken to what looked like a small cafe to eat. There was one table and four chairs. We were served an amazing breakfast. Pancakes, omelets, (no hash browns of course) and cereal. I didn't realize how hungry I was until I smelled the food. I could see by their expressions that the others felt the same way.

One of two of the Council members came as we were finishing up eating. They introduced themselves. Grainne (GRAW nya) which I would later learn means "she who inspires terror." She was Donnchadh's counterpart, they were both military leaders. Accompanying her was Solas (SOH lus) one of the domestic front his name as he informed us means joy, comfort, and solace.

As Solas spoke Grainne's cable eyes rolled. Evidently, she was annoyed with this protocol of name definition. Under her breath I heard her say, "As if anyone cares."

Ah, I thought, dissension among the ranks. I am not sure how that was going to help us, but I had heard it in an old war movie my grandpa was watching.

Grainne interrupted, "We are going to have a Council meeting to determine questions you will be required to answer. Solas and the Two will escort you to the quarters prepared for you. You will each be brought for interro...."

Solas spoke up, "You will each be questioned separately and then as a group. Your..."

"Your fate," Grainne said, living up to her name, "will be determined." Turning abruptly, she walked away.

The words shocked us. Evidently it showed on our faces. Solas consoled, " The Council is balanced and decisions are fair. Beathag is presiding and this is good." His tone changed as he continued. "The Two will escort you to your quarters." He bobbed toward the doorway where Grainne had exited. There stood the two.

They turned as we approached. We followed them to where and what we did not know.

CHAPTER 6

DEJA-VIEW

Awestruck, we walked forward into our accommodations. Looking around it looked like a showroom from a furniture store. It was all one room. In one corner was a refrigerator and cupboards. On the opposite side were two bunk beds with matching bedspreads. At the end of the beds were four shelves with clothes neatly stacked. Four pairs of shoes lined the floor in front of the shelves.

We exchanged looks of disbelief. How did they do this? A click was heard behind us as a television screen was lowered remotely from the ceiling. "No signal," The Two said in unison.

First of the Two continued, "No signal, only DVD's appropriate for your age."

We nodded. "How did you do this?"

"Our technology department is quite advanced," The Second of the Two answered, adding, "We have no idea how they did this."

Jules interrupted, "What do we call you?

"There is no need for you to call us. We will monitor you to assess your needs. "The First offered.

"No, no, I mean do you two have names?" Avery clarified.

"Names, oh, we are at service to you, you need not know our names." We nodded in confused acknowledgement.

"We must call you something...it is wrong for us not to address you by your names." Daichi pleaded.

"We must go, please remain within the perimeter of this space. There are ones with hostility to your presence. You are safe here." With that they stepped beyond the perimeter and a glass partition slid across the entrance.

Jules suggested, "We will call the shorter one First and the taller one Second since that's the order they spoke to us."

Dazed at our predicament we nodded in agreement. I mean, we may not ever see them again so to debate about what to call them seemed futile.

Daichi and I laid eyes on the fridge at the same moment. We raced toward it as Avery hugged Jules. Jules kissed him gently on his cheek and grabbed his hand pulling him to the kitchen area. "I am starving."

Daichi had pulled out most of the contents of the fridge and put them on the kitchen table before Jules and Avery joined us. Jules opened the cupboard door and got four glasses out. "Hand me that juice," she commanded. I abided by her command.

"Avery, make me a sandwich, too. I am pouring juice." Jules justified.

"AAAAvery, make me a sandwich, too, "Daichi said mockingly.

Jules thumped him on the arm. He laughed.

Sandwiches made and half eaten before we realized we had not washed our hands. We all stopped for a moment when Avery brought it to our attention. We nodded and kept on eating. As the last bite of our sandwiches were taken, Avery immediately began making more sandwiches. He handed them off to each of us. Halfway through my stomach began to throb. I had to lean back in the chair for a minute to let my stomach catch up with my mouth.

As I recuperated from my binge, there were pretzels, chocolate cake and two glasses of milk that I didn't mention. "I wonder how they are going to monitor our needs?" I said half to myself.

"That sounds creepy, they are probably listening to us right now." Daichi commented as he scanned the walls for signs of cameras or microphones.

"I think we should clean up and try to sleep," Avery said.

"To heck with cleaning up, let's just go to sleep." Daichi said as he was already heading to the lower bunk of one of the beds. With our stomachs full to the point that it hurt to move, the rest of us followed, Avery making weak protests as he put the perishables in the fridge and joined us. "We can figure things out when we get up." Avery said sleepily as he dragged himself up the ladder to the top bunk over the bed Jules had already slipped into.

Figure what out? I thought. Things are being figured out by our hosts. I think we were all thinking the same thing. From what I could figure we had a bleak future if that chip in my backpack was found and tested. It would give cause to those seeking to avenge the horrors at the hands of humans. Hopefully, it had crumbled into genetically unrecognizable dust. Though I wanted to tell the others and share my panic I didn't since we were being closely monitored.

Once we woke, Jules was the first to take a shower. The air became perfumed with a mixture of scents from shampoo, bath gel, conditioner, and lotion. Avery, Daichi, and I looked through DVDs. Goosebumps was the one we chose. These Potahs had game! Goosebumps was not even in the theaters. They had a bootleg copy. The Potahs were bootleggers. That didn't stop us from watching it. I mean who would we report it to? My thoughts were obviously a result of delirium. I sat back on the couch and watched the movie. Daichi sat on the floor leaning against the couch. He took off his shoes. The stench filled the air. Avery and I pulled the neck of our tee shirts up over our noses.

"Dude, really? Really!" Avery protested.

"Damn, Daichi, did something die in your shoes?" I added. (Sorry Mom. Yes, my mom would consider d*** a curse word.)

"It's not that bad." Daichi defended.

"Uh, yes, yes, it is that bad. Dude." Avery answered back.

"Take them over there," I pointed to a far-off corner. As I spoke, I heard a fan start. The air swirled gently around us, filling the air with a pleasant scent. Really cool or really creepy, Avery and I looked at Daichi then at each other. Daichi started to set his shoes back down.

"No way, dude, no way," Avery interjected, "they still need to get on over to that corner."

"Yeah, no way, put 'em over there," I said as I pulled my shirt down from my nose.

"Funny," Daichi said in reference to our nose filtering. He then whispered as he passed us, "they are monitoring us."

"Ya think?" I asked sarcastically. I rolled my eyes and looked over at Avery who was more annoyed with my arrogance than Daichi's stating the obvious.

"We will figure this out." Avery assured us as he pushed play on the remote control. "Goosebumps" absorbed our attention. Jules joined us. Avery attempted to snuggle up to her. "You need to take a shower," she jokingly pinched her nose shut and laughed. I scooted away from Jules and curled up on my end of the couch as if their love cooties were contagious.

Daichi got up, "I am going to take a quick shower," he said as he walked toward the shelf to get his fresh clothes.

"No, dude. Take a long shower," Avery and Jules high fived me, showing appreciation for my comment.

"You are a comedian," Daichi commented, then asked Jules, "Where'd you get a towel?"

"There in a basket by the tub." She answered in a lullaby voice, she smelled like sweet lavender, just like my mom.

My heart fell and my stomach twisted. This was the first time I had a chance to really think about home. Tears welled in my eyes, one rolled down my cheek. Jules noticed, she handed me a Kleenex, the Potahs had thought of everything. Blowing my nose, I wadded the tissue up and dabbed my eyes with a clean corner. I know I should have dabbed my eyes first, but I was emotionally drained and didn't care if I smeared boogers, well, yes, I did.

My mind is rambling, I went into the kitchen area and sat at the dinette set that looked like my grandmother's. It was pink Formica with chrome legs, the chairs were low back and upholstered in pink vinyl. My eyes wandered; the appliances were avocado green. I decided to get a snack. I opened the freezer and there were those ancient aluminum ice trays with the handle. My mom found some at a thrift store and you would have thought she found a baseball signed by Babe Ruth.

I found out the hard way that cold aluminum bonds with skin when I ripped two layers off of my fingers while getting ice out of the Captain Crunch thing. (Mom says this instead of cussing, she says it a lot.) Only after the layers were ripped off did my dad tell me next time to run warm water over it.

The freezer was full of frozen pizza, duh, imagine that frozen pizza in the freezer, I am such a dweeb. Ice cream, Jimmy Dean sausage biscuits, Dibs, hamburger patties, fish sticks, this was my mother's worst nightmare and my dream come true. I moved the box of sausage finding Pastry Strudel and Bomb pops, the ones with the gum at the top. Yes, my mother's worst nightmare.

Intrigued I opened the refrigerator door as I closed the freezer, there was milk, Sunny Delight, Pepsi, A&W Root Beer, American cheese slices, olives, huge dill pickles, eggs, stuff for sandwiches, just about any kind of chocolate candy you can imagine and cake, a deep dark Devil's Food cake, thick with buttercream icing. My favorite and cottage cheese. Cottage cheese? Oh well they got the rest of it right. It looked like a marketing campaign airing during Saturday morning cartoons.

Cereal, I wonder what kind of cereal they got us? Mom has to be in a very rare mood to buy anything but Corn Flakes, Cheerios, or Rice Krispies. Opening the cabinet next to the fridge there were Lucky Charms, Captain Crunch, the real kind, I wasn't swearing, Cocoa Puffs, Frosted Mini Wheats, Cookie Crunch and Frosted Corn Flakes. On the next shelf were hot Cheetos, Doritos, Fritos, hot fudge, frosted Animal Crackers, and salsa.

I decided to start my food frenzy with cereal and work my way through the rest methodically. Later I would find out from the Two that the scientists studied commercials to learn of our culture and mistakenly got some footage from the '70s and 50's mixed up with current stuff which is where the funky kitchen came from. After eating breakfast, lunch and dinner all in one setting I felt my stomach rumble and realized maybe this wasn't such a good idea. Slowly walking to the couch, I plopped down with a huge sigh, belching from the carbonation of the Pepsi, Root Beer combination that had tasted so good a few minutes ago. The other three were in the kitchen eating at a much more sensible pace, though Daichi's portions were ginormous.

I picked up the remote off the coffee table and propped my feet up in place of it. Without much enthusiasm I flipped through the stations. My stomachache made me appreciate my mother's moderation of my food intake. I guess there was a reason she was so strict. Wizards of Waverly

Place was where I stopped. It was an episode I had seen a few gazillion times, but I watched it anyway.

Jules noticed, "Avery, look your baby brother is watching Disney channel." The three of them said in high pitched unison, "Aww, how cute, did Joshie find his favorite show?" It wasn't the first time they had done this, so they were able to give a scripted response, "Do you want us to get your footsie pajamas and your Teddy bear? "

I raised my hand extending my pinky, mom did this instead of giving people "the finger." She would have knocked me upside the head if she saw me even do this since it was a modification of the other gesture. Avery almost fell off his chair laughing, the other two had no idea what had just happened. I began laughing too, my belly hurt so bad, I felt like it was about to burst.

"Hey, wait!" Avery interrupted. "How are you getting the Disney Channel? The Two said there was no signal." The remote was ripped from my possession and Avery began scrolling to see what else might be on.

Recovering my composure, "Maybe there is a news channel that is reporting on our disappearance!" I excitedly exclaimed. We all looked around to see if our observation had been observed. Sure enough, the sliding door opened and there stood the Two accompanied by a large Russet who demanded we hand over the remote. He changed the channel back to the movie and handed Daichi a remote just for the DVD player.

All day we took turns being anxious about our situation. Avery and Daichi made it seem like they were concerned about Jules and I. Jules pretended to be concerned over me. I, well, I made no bones about being concerned with me. Distraction was good. We played video games and cards. Still tired from our adventure we ended up watching videos from our bunk beds. Once Jules was in bed with fresh blankets up to her chin, Avery leaned over to kiss her goodnight. I was too tired to even say anything obnoxious to them. I now understand the saying, "I fell asleep as soon as my head hit the pillow."

A rumbling sound woke me. It was the same sound that preceded the implosion creating the sink hole. I dived under the bunk bed Jules was now sitting on. Avery was sitting on the couch. Both were stunned. I hollered at them, "Wake up Daichi and get under something." Avery shook Daichi awake. Daichi and Avery dived under the bunk where Daichi had been sleeping. Jules ducked under the bed with me. The rumbling continued for what seemed an eternity.

The swag lamps in the 70's motif kitchen swung back and forth with each violent shock. Then as quickly as it started it stopped. In turtle fashion. I stuck my neck out to survey the situation. The swag lamps were swaying but losing momentum. Nothing else had moved, the vase on the shelf above the TV should have crashed to the ground. It was really weird. My surveying stopped and I followed Jules out from under the bed. Daichi and Avery were already up and looking around as I had been. We were all startled when the entryway door, if you can call a moving glass wall a door, slid open. Watching with anticipation (I was waiting to be busted for the potato chip).

The Two came in a whirlwind of motion, as my grandmother would have said. They were talking to one another, embroiled in another of their continuing debates. Avery stepped over to them. Daichi in agitation, his voice booming across the room, asked, "What is with you two?" The Two stood stunned for a moment and then turned their chaotic chatter to us. Talking over one another, just a few words could be deciphered.

Avery stepped between Daichi and the two. Avery spoke, "Slow down, what is it, what is going on?"

"Yeah," I added in a tone of indignation.

The First of the Two put their hand up to hush the other and began to calmly explain something that once it was explained I wish it hadn't been explained.

After listening to the details, my stomach wrenched in knots. Looking over at Jules and the others I was not alone. The words kept replaying in my mind. They had found the chip and the laboratory concluded that it was one of the decoy chips created by the Potahs. They decided since we had this with us that we must be spies.

"Decoy chips?" Jules asked. "What do you mean, decoy chips?"

The First of the Two began to explain, the other abruptly interrupted. "No time for this, there are more urgent matters." The Second continued. "The Russets are busy clearing debris from the implosion."

The First of the Two interrupted, "Did you guys feel it?" He asked with enthusiasm.

"Yeah, it was cool, nothing broke," I answered.

The disconcerting looks we received shut us both up. We each took a step back and focused on the matter at hand. The First of the Two finished what was to be said.

Jules responded in her clinical manner, one semester of intro to psychology and she is Dr. Phil "If I hear you correctly, the consensus of the council is that we are involved in espionage."

Avery interrupted. "You guys think we are spies and you are going to kill us?"

The Two stammered in unison, "No, no we don't think you are guilty, or anyway that doesn't matter, we and many of us are tired of living for revenge." Calmer, the First continued, "There are many of us, but we are a silent majority, everyone is fearful. Time is wasting. I will tell you what to do and we must do it fast before the Russets come back."

"Wait, what about the Queen, she seemed like she was on our side, her and the peaceable one, you know..." I urged them to think about the Council meeting we had.

"The chip changes all of that. They have no ground to support you now. They are peaceable only until it involves the safety of the Potahs." The Second of the Two explained.

"But then why are you..." my question was hushed by all.

"Shut up and listen," Avery's voice was cutting.

"Wait, can't they hear what we are saying?" I asked urgently.

"No, we took the observation team some soil muck laced with a sleeping agent. We have limited time." The Second of the Two responded in an excited whisper.

The Two shared in telling us the plan as we followed them out the door. As I left the room. I turned for one last look. There was nothing in the room, it was a cave with dirt floors. That blew my mind, where did everything go so quickly? I started to ask, but as I raised my voice, I was met with a hostile glare from Avery. I opened my mouth to speak again, and Jules shushed me. I decided to listen to what the Two were saying. I found out some bizarre stuff.

Implosions were done to access the huge freezers of fast-food warehouses. The Potahs had mastered mass hypnosis aided by holographic imagery. (That explains the disappearance of the stuff in the room.) Using these tools, a team of elite Potahs set out to project the first Golden Arches on the surface of the Earth. Ideally, the implosion would cut down the burrowing time to enter the freezer. The Russets led the tunneling brigade, which consisted of all able bodied Potahs. Each had their assignment from actual tunneling to carrying water and setting up rest stations.

As the First relayed this, Avery interrupted, "How come you guys aren't involved?"

The Second of the Two answered, "We lagged behind and then turned around so we could help you. With the urgency of the work even if they missed us they will dismiss it until the project is done, which usually takes almost two sleep cycles." (They didn't have a sun and moon, so this meant two days.) As the Two continued on with their explanation, I could not help but think that these Potahs were risking their lives for us. What would happen to them after we were gone? I began to ask but as I opened my mouth, I was assaulted by eye daggers from Avery and Jules. I returned my evilest look back to him, but I did keep quiet.

The First of the Two continued with the story explaining once an elite team of Russets, (I guess it would be their version of the Navy Seals) burrowed through to the foundation they used an explosive with just enough force to break an area just large enough for the team of Potahs to pass through.

Once in there they had little time to add genetically altered chips in the form of French fries to each box of frozen fries. They then taped the box shut and no one was the wiser. The chemists designed an expanding putty to fill in the hole after them which dried as cement. The tunnel would remain intact for future missions. Despite the icy stares, I asked about the chip in my backpack.

The First of the Two answered. "In the nineteen seventies we created several new holographs to be imitated, stackable chips were one of them."

I felt kinda bad. I didn't speak up about their safety, but I did about a potato, or a non-potato chip. It wasn't right.

The Potahs began to guide us into the tunnel. Avery asked, "Why do they alter the potatoes to poison us?"

"Oh, my no," The Second of the Two spoke, "Oh, more sinister than that, they want to stagnate you, they want you to become...."

"Couch potatoes!" Daichi interjected.

CHAPTER 7

FROZEN ASSETS

"Yes," the Two acknowledged with a bob of their bodies. They had stopped moving as the conversation started.

"So, let me get this straight," Avery began to speak, but was interrupted by the Second of the Two. "Come on, we must proceed.'

"Yes," the First of the Two answered and continued talking as we hurriedly made our way, "We have to get to the top of the tunnel at just the right time. Oh, and we all want to preserve our energy from here on out. It is a tough climb."

We entered the ancillary tunnel, a tunnel dug alongside the main tunnel so the Potahs can easily tunnel into this tunnel and escape disaster should one occur. We sunk our feet into the footholds on each side of the tunnel and began climbing. I was amazed at how good the Potahs were at this. They rhythmically rooted their way up like they were swimming in water. Then it occurred to me, this was their natural habitat. My mind whirled around the events of the last twenty-four hours.

A wheezing whisper caught my attention. "Hey," the beleaguered voice of Jules said, "you guys do realize we are seeking sanctuary in a deep freezer." We continued climbing. It hadn't occurred to me that we were exchanging one dire circumstance for another. I was just thinking of being on the Topside, as the Potahs called it.

"No talking!" The First of the Two commanded in a hushed whisper, pointing to the wall of the tunnel indicating there was not much room between us and the other Potahs. Solemnly we continued to climb. Imagining we looked like crabs or spiders inching our way up the tunnel walls kept my mind occupied as fatigue consumed me. Loosened dirt caked my hair and fell onto my face. Sweat caused streaks of dirt to line my skin. Licking my lips left me with a mouth full of dust, misery.

Daichi began using the top of his head to boost me along as my energy ran low. He was taking this in stride, after all he was an All-Star defensive end. Avery looked down at me, my face a smeared mud fest and asked in a whisper, "Joshie, you gonna be okay?"

I nodded. Thank goodness I wasn't allergic to dirt. Jules was ahead of Avery and her pace caused each of us to slow too. In all honesty, it was not just Jules that slowed our pace, Avery was running out of steam too. I couldn't complain since Daichi took up my slack. I guess it was handy to have the Neanderthal with us.

The Two finally stopped. Their cable eyes bore into the dirt between us and the Russets stopping just shy of going all the way through. They assessed the progress of the mission. The Second of the Two gave the okay signal we took that to mean things were unfolding as they should. A nervous shudder ran through me as I imagined what the near future held. The Two, I never got to ask what would become of the Two. I would soon find out.

We felt an explosion! Loosened dirt and small rocks slid down past us to the tunnel floor, well most of it passed us. We heard urgent voices and movement from the other side of the wall. We were then instructed by the First of the Two that we had to get between the last Russet coming out and the sealing of the hole. That meant we would have to burrow almost through to the other tunnel, wait for the last Russet to return to their tunnel, shove the last bit of dirt out of our way, and climb into the freezer while keeping the Russets from getting to us.

My stomach dropped. I think I know why the Two did not tell us the plan. This was crazy. We were supposed to all get into the freezer and keep the Navy Seals of the Potahs at bay. How were we going to do that? I hope the Two had something up their sleeve that we didn't know about.

The Second one of the Two said something to the One. With a strong voice the Second one of the Two said, "One, two, three, push." We all pushed on the tunnel wall between the Russets and us. The wall began to crumble, we heard voices from the other side. We dug as we pushed, our fingers raw. The final clump of Earth fell away. The First of the Two entered the tunnel feet first, pushing down on the unsuspecting Russet. Then Jules went, she used the Second Potah as support to shimmy her way into the freezer. Daichi let the Second shimmy past him in the tunnel and up into the freezer.

Daichi had seen the First of the Two bob up and down as the Russets fought to stop us. Avery, then I made it up into the freezer. Daichi reached down to help the First of the Two climb up just as a Russet grabbed the First's leg. Daichi reached back for the First's hand and pulled heartedly. The force caught the Russet by surprise and the First of the Two was jerked loose from the Russett's grasp, but it also caused the First to lose footing. Daichi reached down again and grabbed the First by a bundle of cable eyes. A shriek of pain echoed through the now adjoining tunnels. The First was able to gain footing and Daichi could reach his outstretched hand.

Daichi grasped the hand with both of his and let out a deep grunt as he pulled with every ounce of his strength the First up to where the footholds could support him. Suddenly, the First jerked. The Russet had shot a poisoned dart into the starchy flesh of the First. Daichi tugged with adrenaline filled strength. But the limp weight of the First was too much for Daichi to hold onto. With all the energy he could muster, the First pushed against the footing blocking the tunnel from the ensuing Russets. Looking down the tunnel I could see a sea of cable eyes swarming like hornets. The Russets were gaining on us. The First was grabbed by the leg as Daichi climbed into the freezer, Avery grabbed his hand and with a jerk that landed Avery on his butt Daichi was pulled to safety. He turned to reach out to the First. but it was too late. The poisonous dart had taken effect and the First was tumbling down onto the Russets creating a clear escape for us. Jules was mixing the chemical compound that would seal the tunnel from the pursuing Potahs.

We heard screams echo up from the tunnel. The screams chilled us more than the freezer. We all thought of the First. Tears welled in our eyes. He saved us. The Second looked over at Jules, clearing his throat and regaining his composure, he nodded to Jules to seal the tunnel. There was nothing more we could do for the First. He died with honor, and we would never forget his sacrifice. However, the Second told us that the lead Russet would suffer a fate worse than death if he survived and if he died those who bore his name would be shamed. The fate worse than death was to be denounced as a warrior. For lesser crimes than defaulting in duty he would be ostracized. For letting us go and interfering with our capture he would have to wear a wet burlap bag which would slowly cause him to rot. The stench would cause others to shun him. The Second had only seen this punishment once and it was horrific. The Second shuddered as the words were spoken.

As these details were related to us, Jules applied the mixture with the instructions the First laboriously supplied. Jules filled the hole. The Second took Jules hands in hers and spit, rubbing it into her hands caked with the mixture. This really grossed Jules out, but it was necessary to neutralize the chemicals so it would not burn into her skin. After rubbing her hands for a moment, she wiped them on her sweatshirt. We turned our attention to the Second. He was oozing starch from the cable eyes that were torn entering the freezer. The Second instructed us on how to soothe the pain. It was more than just cable eyes, the Second explained. He had also sustained bruises under the thick outer skin. The Second made a salve out of dirt and spit and instructed Avery to smooth it onto the injuries. Avery reluctantly complied. The Second was sullen. No one knew what to say to him about the loss of the First. Jules sat with her arm as far as it could reach around the Second.

We huddled around them. We found out that the Potahs are not only resistant to the cold but have an internal antifreeze that radiates warmth. All kinds of thoughts ran through my mind. What would happen to the Second once we were discovered topside? I shuddered as the image of King Kong on the Empire State Building flashed in my mind. Would they believe us that the Potahs are infusing the frozen French fry supplies? How are we going to get home? Will we be put in juvie for breaking and entering?

The Second began to cool down. My fingers were blue and numb as were my ears and nose. Icicles formed on my nose hairs, and I felt so sleepy. Avery saw me drifting off and he flicked my frozen ear, "Ahhhh!" I cried out in pain. "No way Joshie you gotta stay awake!" Jules was looking over at us with glassy eyes, like she was seeing right through us. Daichi shifted around sluggishly.

I visualized sunny beaches, the Mojave Desert at a hundred fourteen degrees. Volcanoes erupting, a blazing fire, a hot bath, drinking hot cocoa. My thoughts were interrupted by the seal of the freezer door breaking open. A light went on overhead. Two voices were heard, there was laughing. I could hear the footsteps as they drew closer. We were so frozen that we could barely move, but we needed to draw attention to us, which I don't know what I was worried about since we were huddled around a ginormous potato.

"Hey, hey, what is this!" One of the men said. The other one turned, "What's wha" He stopped mid-sentence. The first employee spoke, "What are they doing here?"

In an agitated tone the second employee spoke, as he hurried toward us, "We won't ever find that out if we don't get them outta here. Get over here, now!"

The first employee joined the other. Together they helped each of us out of the freezer. When they got to the Potah they looked dumbfounded at each other. They started to walk out, leaving the Second behind. Daichi sprung up and pushed past the two of them. He helped the Second up. He was in better shape then we were warmth wise. He lumbered out of the freezer. The warehouse rumbled with noise of work being done with forklifts and people hollering. The open doors to the warehouse allowed rays of sun to shine in. The Potah began bobbing and chanting.

"It is the trail of the gods." Whispered the Second.

Then he went on to elaborate in the same reverent tone. "We have legends about the trail of the gods. We are fearful. We are too close to the gods."

My attention was drawn away. The first employee, who had the name Gerald embroidered on his shirt, told the second, Wesley, to call 911 as he handed us blankets. Wesley stood frozen staring at the Potah who had stopped bobbing as he listened to Avery explain about the sun, careful not to dismiss his original reaction.

"Now! Get your cell out and call 911. Never mind, just gimme your phone!" Gerald demanded of Wesley. Wesley handed over his phone without taking his eyes off the Potah. Daichi had wrapped a blanket around the Second.

The sting of my extremities thawing was almost unbearable. I thought of what my grandma had told me about wearing a hat. If your head is cold the body will take blood which circulates heat from the feet and hands to warm the head, so the brain keeps receiving oxygen. I pulled the blanket I was given up over my head and waited for my body to warm. I looked over at the other three. How do we explain the Potah? My mind began whirling with ideas.

I was stirred back to reality as the warmth from a space heater blew across my face. Finally, the feeling of life began to flow through me, warm and comforting. The sound of sirens and then tires screeching to a stop ripped me back into reality. So many car doors slammed that I lost count. They were coming for us! I heard voices getting nearer and nearer. I heard the crackling of radios. Another set of sirens stopped and another door to the warehouse rolled up. An ambulance did a three point turn and backed in. The paramedics assessed the scene as they calmly walked toward us.

Behind them thundering footsteps drew closer and closer. Once these people reached us, they stood back as we were examined. It was determined that, surprise, surprise we were suffering from hypothermia and dehydration. Another layer of blankets were added to each of us and IV's were started.

"Who is your buddy?" A woman from the mystery group asked.

There was no waiting for a response, she continued. "A Potah, I have only read about these creatures."

The way she said "these creatures" was like that old movie, *Creature of the Black Lagoon*. It creeped me out and made me mad. "The Second is not a creature. Potah, a good Potah, who helped us escape."

"Joshie, thank you, I will take it from here." She directed her attention toward the Second.

The Second's cable eyes rose and watched the others in the group. He then addressed the woman, "Is it not customary for one to introduce oneself before entering into a conversation?"

"I am detective Florez." She said sternly.

Showing no emotion, she asked how we all ended up in the freezer.

The Second started to recall the details of our escape. The rest of the detectives were milling around the warehouse, a few went into the freezer gathering evidence, though I don't know what they thought they would find more evidential than the Second.

Two shiny black sedans came to a screeching halt on either side of the ambulance. They had to be FBI, I know because Florez said, "There's the FBI."

Florez met the first pair of agents as they rose from the car. Curtly they introduced themselves. They then walked right over to us. One of the second pair of agents began talking to detective Florez in hushed tones.

The other asked the Second to stand. Daichi helped steady him. The other agent who was talking to detective Florez left her and joined in the interrogation of the Potah. Before they could begin one of the other agents came over and said, "We have been instructed by the Pentagon to bring all four of the kids to the Capital. The Chief of Staff has taken a personal interest. The CIA will take care of the creature once we get to Washington, DC,"

"The Chief of Staff, wasn't that the President?" I asked Avery to be sure, Avery nodded, not taking his eyes off the FBI agents.

The CIA and the Second. This made me uncomfortable. Images of King Kong on the top of the Empire State Building flooded my mind. Then King Kong turned into the Second. I shuddered. It had not occurred to me that the government would be interested or even know about the Potahs. The First and Second had rescued us. The First even sacrificed herself for us. Panic filled me as my mind raced thinking of horrible things that could happen to the Second. I was so worried that it did not sink into my brain that we were going to the White House, or I supposed that would be where we would be taken. I mean that is where the President is, right?

Agent Florez went to the paramedics to check on our condition. I looked down at my fingers which were now sensitive but warm. The paramedic reported we were stable but needed continued rehydration. The lead paramedic said we should see a doctor within twenty-four hours to make sure everything was fine, but there was no need to take us to the hospital. The paramedics and their driver acted like it was normal to see giant talking potatoes. They never asked one question.

The White House had a doctor, I remembered that from a report I had done. The paramedics removed our IV's and were assured we would be treated by a doctor within twenty-four hours. A large black van, as shiny as the sedans that pulled into the entrance of the now crowded warehouse. Looking around I saw the warehouse was empty, I mean the employees were gone. The two employees that found us were talking with the first pair of agents. They both nodded in agreement that they were not to talk of this to anyone. Gerald said, "Like, who would believe us anyway." Then Wesley added, "Yeah, who would believe us. I am not sure I believe it." There was no change in the agent's demeanor. The employees shook their extended hands and scurried away.

The FBI agents thanked the paramedics and the detective for their service, after signing affidavits swearing secrecy regarding "the situation surrounding these circumstances." The agent that did most of the talking up to this point sent them on their way saying, "We will take it from here."

There was an uneasy silence as the ambulance was boarded by the paramedics. It was only after the detective's car backed away from the building that the agents spoke.

A brief discussion ensued amongst them; we were told that two of us would ride in each sedan. The van's doors were open wide to accommodate the Second. The Potah was nervously chattering in Gaelic under his breath and tears starched his face. It was not a regular sized van. It was more like a large, armored truck like what they pick up money from the banks in. I was relieved when Daichi spoke up, "Could I go in the van, I mean if there is room? I think the Potah would do better, respectfully." He bowed slightly, to convey his sincerity directing his request to the female agent. She went over to the other agents to confer. After a short minute, she nodded over to Daichi. This meant one of us would be alone, I looked pleadingly at Avery. He rolled his eyes at me, and then asked the agent standing closest to us if it was okay if the three of us rode in one car. The agents easily agreed to the request without any discussion.

The driver of the van lowered a lift so the Second could be, well, lifted. Daichi followed behind the Second holding his back to help him keep his balance. I could see Daichi sitting on the bench beside the Second.

The agents that we were riding with each opened a rear car door for us to get in. Jules and Avery entered from one side and me from the other.

Jules was in the middle. "Belt up," the male agent instructed. We complied. As we backed out of the warehouse following behind the van and the other sedan following us, Agents Theresa Brooks and Vern Sinclair introduced themselves officially. We then told them our names, which they already knew. As we drove, we talked about living in California, in the Mojave desert and just about everything about us. The agents revealed little about themselves but kept the conversation flowing by asking us a bajillion questions. The only thing they didn't ask us was about the implosion and being with the Potahs.

After about two hours in the car, I had to go pee and I was starving. I whispered to Jules. Jules nodded, took a deep breath and spoke. "Um, excuse me, um we need to use the bathroom and if there is any way we could get some food, we would appreciate it?" The second part was one of those half questions, half statements.

Agent Sinclair slapped his forehead with the butt of his hand. "How awful of us, Brooks, these kids are hungry, of course," He looked over at Jules for the second half of the statement. "Next exit, let's get something, I'll radio the others to let them know we are stopping."

"Should we stop or just drive through? Piper and Findley have to stay with their vehicle." Brooks responded.

"Hell, they can wait on us, we have waited on them plenty of times." Sinclair responded. "How many times will these kids get to hang with the FBI?" I could see his smile in the rear-view mirror.

How cool is that! We are going to have, I guess it was lunchtime, lunch with the FBI. They had their jackets folded over the back of the front seat. I inched forward as much as I could with my seatbelt on and saw Sinclair's gun. Maybe people would think we were dangerous juveniles, so bad the local law couldn't contain us or maybe they would think we were undercover agents posing as kids. My mind continued to create unlikely scenarios. We went into a Cracker Barrel alongside the interstate. We were in Tennessee.

"When do we get to see our parents?" I asked Brooks as I exited the car. Tears welled in my eyes and my voice cracked despite my attempts to be stoic.

Brooks put her hand on my shoulder and turned me, so I looked straight into her eyes, "Your parents are being flown out to Washington,

D.C. as we speak. You will most likely see them, let's see, we will be driving all night, by tomorrow night." Her dark brown eyes shone with sincerity. Then she straightened up, and out of habit, she assessed her surroundings. As she guided me to the door of the restaurant, she continued to scan the premises. Daichi jumped down from the van. The agent shut the door and walked over with him to meet us. I guessed this wasn't Piper when she said, "Hey get Piper and me burgers, onion rings, and Cokes. No, wait Piper drinks Pepsi and he wants fries." Sinclair nodded. Findley started back to the van.

Feeling emboldened I turned to this agent and introduced myself, "Hello, I am Joshua Durbin, but everyone calls me Josh." I left off the "e." With all I am going through I no longer felt like Joshie, I would now be Josh, well to everyone but my mom.

"Well, hello Josh Durbin, I am Agent Rebecca Findley." She said with mock propriety. She covered the ground between us and extended her hand. We shook. She then returned to the van.

I opened the door for Agent Brooks. She smelled really nice, kinda like my mom did right after she got out of the shower. She thanked me for opening the door and chided the male agents about chivalry.

"You carry your own gun; you open your own doors." Sinclair retorted.

"The Second is really upset," Gerald said as we sat down in the oversized booth.

Jules said with tears in her eyes and emotion in her voice, "We really need to be sympathetic to the Second, he is so sensitive. And, well after what happened to the First."

"The First?" Brooks asked in a hushed voice.

"The First, well, died helping us escape." Avery answered choking back tears, "They were the first two Potahs we saw. They were like twins. They were always together and in the beginning we just saw them as two. Then we began to see that they were very connected but definitely separate personalities. So, we would say, First of the Two and the Second of the Two. Over time we saw that the First was the stronger personality and the Second relied on the First. So, we referred to them as the First of the Two and the Second of the Two, then just called them the First and the Second."

I must have been daydreaming because Jules elbowed me in the ribs, "The server asked you what you want to eat."

"Oh," I looked down at the menu. "I want a cheeseburger and fri. No onion rings and a chocolate malt, oh, and a glass of water, please." The agents laughed when I changed my order to onion rings instead of fries.

"That's a hungry young man," Brooks smiled at me. I wanted to ask her a million questions about what had happened and what was going to happen. Realizing it was better not to know most of the answers. I needed to stop thinking and enjoy the moment, that is what Grandpa always tells me. Grandpa, tears welled in my eyes. I pinched them away with my fingers and sniffed as quietly as I could. The agents continued to scan the crowd, though Brooks glanced over at me.

When the food came it was all business, no more chit chatting. We ate and then left; the agents were back in agent mode the minute we got up from the table. I went to the restroom one more time before getting back in the car. Brooks took food out for Piper and Findley. Daichi took two large "to go" cups of water for the Second. Findley opened the door and let Daichi in the back of the van. Piper signaled Findley that something was up. Findley tossed the food into the van and let the soft drinks fall on the ground. She drew her gun and with her back against the van she eased her way into the van. Piper shifted in reverse and left the parking lot. The other agents hurried us into the sedan and both sedans screeched out of the parking lot following the van back onto the interstate.

Findley radioed Brooks to answer her cell phone. The cell rang. Brooks listened as Findley talked. Brooks simply said, "We have you covered."

Brooks nudged Sinclair's elbow indicating for him to pull in front of the van. Briefly they exchanged glances. As our sedan moved in front of the van the other sedan pulled close up to the rear of the van which was now going down the interstate at ninety miles an hour. My heart began beating intensely with the excitement. Were we out running terrorists or were kidnappers out to get the Potah?

"Damn," Brooks said, "I knew we should have detained the witnesses of the Potah." My heart warmed when she said Potah and not the creature. "We should have isolated them and debriefed them."

"The Pentagon only wanted signed affidavits. They will handle this once we get there." Sinclair added.

"Are they okay?" Jules asked.

"Everything is fine, someone must have told the press about the Potah." Sinclair turned to Brooks, "Had to be one of the employees, maybe the ones that found them." Turning back to Jules, "Nothing serious, Jules, the only shooting we have to worry about is cameras."

Sinclair turned back to Brooks, "Drive throughs from now on and regulated bathroom breaks." Brooks nodded, never taking her eyes off the road.

We drove into the night before we stopped again. While Brooks pumped gas Sinclair escorted us to the restroom. If something happened again Findley and Piper would leave immediately, and the sedans would follow suit once everyone was accounted for. Pictures of us kids could be explained more easily than pictures of the Second.

Things went smoothly. One at a time the agents used the restroom. We were back on the road with a full tank and empty bladders. Within the hour we drove through Hardee's which is Carl's Jr back in California to get dinner. I got one of those chocolate cakes for dessert. When I go with mom to the store, sometimes we sneak and have one before dinner. She swears that if I tell anyone she will deny it to her grave. Oops, I just told. My eyes grew heavy after eating. I smiled as I realized that I just ate fast food in an FBI car. Sinclair did gather all the trash and put it in a plastic trash sack with the FBI insignia on it. I guess the FBI has protocol for everything.

The next thing I remember is the sun shining on my face, drool running down my chin. My neck was stiff. I sat up straight and rotated my head from side to side. Jules was already awake. Avery was just stirring. We were driving over a bridge. The water below was churning. I had to pee, really bad and watching the water wasn't helping.

CHAPTER 8

PENCILVANIA AVENUE

I expressed to the agents that I needed to pee...um no I actually said that I needed to use the restroom. I was assured we would be stopping soon for just that reason. Jules nudged me.

"You read my mind, I have to go too." She then nudged Avery who was resistantly waking up.

"What the," he said in an agitated tone until he realized it was Jules who had woken him. "What's up Jules?" His tone was markedly sweeter.

"Restroom break." Jules informed him.

"We will grab something to eat, too," Agent Sinclair added.

As we got back to the car after our break Brooks told us we would be in the District of Columbia in about two hours. I wondered how we got so far east. I mean we fell into the sinkhole in California. I realized I had said this out loud. Agent Sinclair responded. "We have the same question, Josh."

Most importantly in a few hours I would be seeing my mom and dad. My heart ached for them. I even missed my three- year-old twin sisters. Mom gets mad at me when I say we have been infiltrated by tiny terrorists. Really, if the terrorists wanted to really upset the day-to-day life of Americans, they should give every family twin three- year-olds. A smile formed as I thought of my family. I settled back in my seat.

Avery said what I had been thinking, "Are the twins coming with my parents?"

"No mention of that from headquarters, however, I presume with the seriousness of the circumstances they most likely are at home with a relative." Brooks responded.

Jason, he would be watching them. When I visualized Jason watching the twins, I realized the unique pattern my family had established. Kiera, who was one, was my niece. Making me, of course, her uncle. That doesn't seem so odd. I mean I am a teenager. However, it also meant my three-year- old twin sisters were also her aunts. Then I thought of Ky and Jaden who were eleven and thirteen. I am their uncle, and I am fourteen. It's odd but this is the first time I applied the stereotypical roles of uncles and nieces to these two who had been my besties growing up. We were more like cousins, but I knew I needed to find a way to use my position as uncle to my benefit. My mind came to a screeching halt. How long had I been lost within myself, envisioning these scenarios? And, why, did my mind decide right now to analyze my familial bonds? I shook my head in an effort to reboot my brain back to the present.

I looked at the faces of those around me. I thought they would think I had lost my mind. I realized as I looked at each of them that they too were absorbed in thought. Each of us processing what has happened and projecting on what is yet to come.

To no one and everyone I asked, "What is going to happen to the Potah?" Avery and Jules nodded in agreement. Our eyes fixed on Agent Sinclair. At the sound of my question, Agent Sinclair, who was in the front seat, twisted her torso, enabling her to look us in the eyes as she responded somberly.

"That is out of our hands, Josh."

I turned to face the scenery as it passed to hide the tears welling in my eyes. There were more and more structures, buildings of all sizes. Mesmerized and silent, I could hear Jules and Avery talk in hushed tones. Finally, I put my head back against the seat and closed my eyes. A tear trailed down my face.

After some time, Brooks spoke, "Okay, kids, we are here."

"Where exactly is here?" I looked out the window and answered my own question. The White House, that is where we were.

"We made good time," Brooks announced.

Looking behind me the van carrying the Second and Daichi pulled in behind us then drove past, turning a corner and going to the back of the White House. The other sedan followed. We were let out in the front of the White House like we were heads of state or some celebrity guest. Four Secret Service were waiting for us. Normally I would have said they were there to greet us but there was no greeting involved. There were no introductions. The FBI agents presented their badges. The Secret Service agent that confirmed the identities of Brooks and Sinclair, nodded to the other three of the Secret Service. A tall man came out from the White House to greet us. Now, there were introductions. The man introduced himself as a Colonel in the United States Army. Johnson, Colonel Johnson. There were four Secret Service that joined us as we walked through the White House to a sitting room where we would wait for further instructions. The sitting room had a table full of fruit and sandwiches, juice, and water. A large plate of veggies was next to the plates and glasses. A butler seated us on couches where trays of the food were set next to us. I mindlessly ate as I took in the whole experience. I was so enthralled that I even swallowed a Brussels sprout.

So many thoughts ran through my mind, I wished Daichi was with us. I wondered where he was and how he was handling all of this. Then I was glad for the Second that Daichi was with him, but I still wished he was with us, that both were with us. My parents, where were they? I looked over at the two agents standing at the entrance of the room surveying the situation outside.

Colonel Johnson spoke briefly on the phone and then came over to us. He told us that we would have to wait for a little longer than was anticipated but he would have to excuse himself to take care of some details. As he turned to walk away Jules jumped up from her seat, "Excuse me, before you go, um sir, could you tell me when I can see my brother?" Jules pleaded, "Daichi, my brother was in the van with the Potah, where is he?" The Colonel looked around at the agents by the door. "Well, young lady, that is exactly where I am going right now, to talk to your brother, Daichi, is it?" His voice was abrupt. He turned and left the room.

Jules punched a pillow on the couch as she sat back down, her face was red with fury. "I want to know where Daichi is, damn it," one of the agents glanced over his shoulder to survey the situation. Jules threw one more punch into the pillow beside her and bent forward with her face in her hands.

The agents assigned to us had no reaction to Jules' outburst. She slumped lower into the couch. I went over and sat by her not knowing exactly what to do. Avery joined us and assured her that everything will be fine, but his tone did not indicate full confidence. "Daichi is fine, I'm sure. I mean, we are talking about the U.S. government and not some tyrannical dictatorship, after all." His tone indicated he was attempting to convince himself as well as us. "They are probably still questioning him since he rode with the Second, maybe they think he knows more than the rest of us." Jules wiped her eyes with the back of her hand. One of the agents stepped forward and offered her a handkerchief. Robert De Niro said, in the movie "*The Intern*," that it is a sign of chivalry for a man to carry a handkerchief because the only thing to really use one for is to offer it to a lady that has been crying. And the chivalry includes the fact that once offered to and used, well, you really don't want it back. So, this gesture of offering a handkerchief would result in losing your handkerchief. We had a chivalrous Secret Service agent. Avery and I both nodded and thanked him. Jules took it from his hand, wiped her tears then blew her nose. When she offered it back to the agent, he politely declined.

About an hour passed when a man entered the room. I recognized him as Secretary of State. He spoke to the Secret Service agent by the door, and he came over to us, instructing us to follow them. We did, down a long hallway that turned into a corridor without windows or doors.

Two CIA agents met us. I know because they flashed their badges and said, "CIA." We came to a stop in front of a set of double doors guarded by two uniformed guards. The two CIA agents grabbed each doorknob and opened the doors to reveal the Oval Office to our entourage, minus two of the Secret Service who took posts on the outside of the door, replacing the two that had been on duty prior to us showing up.

My heart beat so hard that I could feel the pounding in my throat as I looked around, finally settling my gaze on the man rising out of his chair behind a large desk. President Obama walked around to greet us. He shook each one of our hands and called us each by name. We were then asked to have a seat on one of the couches that were facing each other. We were all careful not to step on the American Seal between the couches and the president's desk. The president took a seat across from us and the agents stood behind us.

With authority President Obama asked, "Was there not four of these brave young people?"

Agent Brooks answered, "Yes, sir, the fourth, Daichi, who goes by Daichi, rode with the Potah. He should be joining us momentarily."

"So, Joshua, Avery, and Jules, you have been on quite an adventure. Do you have any questions?"

Jules spoke up. "Daichi is okay?"

The President nodded. He looked over toward the Secretary of State. She answered, "Yes, he is on his way as we speak, Mr. President.

President Obama looked at Jules, "Jules?"

Jules nodded and then remembered her manners remembering she was speaking to the President, "Yes, yes President Obama, it does. "

"I just wanted to come by and meet you brave youngsters." The President interjected and then continued. "We are going to have the four of you freshen up and eat, then we will go from there." The President told us in a soothing voice. "Once Daichi joins us, we will take you for the process. We request that you each review in your mind what happened, as many details as possible, though do not speak to each other from this point until we have had a chance to talk with you individually once again."

Daichi was led into the room by an agent I hadn't seen before. I supposed she must be CIA. Another two agents followed. The President shook Daichi's hand and repeated the same thing he had said to us. He excused the CIA agents. They nodded and left without hesitation. The Secretary of State now had President Obama's attention.

"Escort these young people to freshen up. Then meet me back here." He then turned his attention to us, "I will meet with you after you have freshened up. We have a lot to talk about."

In the company of the Secretary of State we were escorted by one of the staff to individual bathrooms. Before Daichi and I parted, he looked at me, and in an undertone said, "I am worried about the Potah. The Second is being treated like a spy."

My heart pounded and my stomach knotted. I whispered back, "President Obama will listen to us." I said with confidence I was surprised I could muster.

Yes, I told myself, the President would understand how the First and Second had saved our lives and how the First even lost its life.

After freshening up we were taken to the patio overlooking the Rose Garden and served lunch. Three Secret Service stood nearby waiting for us. Once we finished eating our lunch, we were whisked away to an elevator that went down to the basement.

In a room with a conference table and chairs, we were asked to take a seat on the near side of the table. There were six intimating figures across from us, none of which was the President. Three were in military uniforms with stars on their shoulders and a lot of medals and ribbons all over the front of their uniform jackets.

The other two were dressed in the blackest suits I had ever seen. They were all about as old as my grandpa and the Secretary of State. The two in the black suits alternated in the questioning while a woman typed like in the court everything anyone said. After stating who we are and where we live, we asked the full names of our parents. One of the black suits looked in the direction of the typist and said, "These are the names of the parents that have given permission for us to debrief the said minors." The typist (which I would learn later was a stenographer) nodded when she completed the disclosure.

Jules was asked to stay and the rest of us were taken to a room, and each given an ancient DS to play. We were instructed by one of the two Secret Service agents not to speak to one another. After about twenty minutes we heard a door down the hall open and close. Though Jules did not come back, an agent came and asked for Daichi to go with her. After about thirty minutes we heard the door open and close again down the hall. This time Avery was asked to go with them. I was glad because I was winning Angry Birds and would have been bummed if I had to stop.

The same process was repeated. The door down the hallway opened and closed and then the agent came for me. I was losing at that point, so I wasn't as upset about stopping. I followed the agent back to the original room. There was a plaque next to the door that read, Debriefing Room A-1. Wow, we were being debriefed like the soldiers when they came back from a mission. That made me feel really important, how many kids could say they had been debriefed by the CIA and generals and the Secretary of State?

I was invited to take a seat. A glass of cold water was set on the table for me to drink if I got thirsty during the process of debriefing, yes debriefing. I was being debriefed. Once I stated my name for the record, I was asked to tell what happened from the morning we fell into the sinkhole until I was brought here to be interviewed. (Ha, they don't think I know I am being debriefed) With careful consideration of each minute detail I recounted all that had happened. The stenographer typed away and the adults all shifted in their chairs as they listened.

An hour and a half later I reunited with the others. Avery looked up at me agitated. "My battery died on the DS twenty minutes ago. How could you spend that much time talking?"

"I have a photographic memory," I said in an aloof tone. "I had more details to share than you.

"You are such a dweeb." His tone was familiarly irritated.

We heard voices in the hallway. Avery looked at us and told us to be quiet so we might hear what was being said.

With his ear against the door Avery listened to the conversation.

It was President Obama talking to another person, probably one of the guys that debriefed us. Avery nodded a few times as he listened. When the voices stopped, we heard footsteps coming down the hall toward the room we were in. Just as the door opened, Avery moved away and told us that the other person said that our stories matched.

The President and one of the two non-military debriefers came into the room. "Thank you all for the time you took to tell us what happened after the sinkhole incident."

Daichi abruptly interjected, "The Potah is not a spy. The Second and First helped save our lives after the scientists found a piece of a potato chip in Joshie's backpack." Pleading, Daichi continued. "The Second will be okay, right? We will be able to see him soon, right?"

The debriefer looked at the President. He finally spoke. "I appreciate your concerns and once the processing is complete, we will consider your requests."

Daichi was not satisfied, "They are treating him like a spy, like he is a threat! After all he did for us, that's just not right!"

The President took Daichi's comments in stride. "It is necessary to follow protocol in this situation. I will make your concerns known to those who are working with the Potah. It is a situation where the security of our country is at stake." His serious tone changed. He continued in what I would call his "father" voice. "You will be taken to have afternoon refreshments and then for the rest of the afternoon my daughters will be ambassadors and show you the fun parts of the White House. Then your parents will join us for dinner."

My mind had been working overtime. At the debriefing it was said that my parents had approved for us to be debriefed. How could they do that if they weren't here yet? So, I asked President Obama. "By fax, we sent the forms and they faxed them back with their signatures."

Malia walked into the room very poised. Sasha bounded into the room with apparent eagerness to meet us. Probably not us but anyone that was new and a potential friend. I wondered how they got to play with friends. I mean no one could come and ring the doorbell to see if they could come out and play. I was sure they must have planned times that they got to see friends. Ms. Michelle would see to that. I did see a picture where the girls were getting into a car and Sasha had a backpack like, well, like a normal kid. I wondered what it would be like to have the President's daughter in your class.

Sasha asked what we wanted to do first. There was a bowling alley, a movie theater, and a basketball court. There was also a swimming pool. The older kids didn't answer quick enough. Sasha and I said bowling at the same time. I mean I am a kid that was cooped up in a car for almost three days. Sasha led the way, walking as fast as she could. I kept up with her. Malia told her to slow down and walk. Her response was, "I am walking, just fast."

We passed Secret Service agents who had to jump out of our way. The one assigned to Sasha was taking long strides to keep up with us, never saying a word. I figured he would tell us to slow down, he was a grown up. Later Sasha would tell us that she and Malia were allowed to behave as they would without the agents around unless they were in mortal danger.

Sasha suddenly slowed down and I followed her lead. I realized why when I saw Ms. Obama was standing in a doorway down the hall. We rode the elevator down to the bowling alley. There were shoes and socks for us to put on, and the games began. The activity distracted me from the Second and kept me from continuing to ruminate about our situation.

After bowling we went to the theater and watched *Brave*. We had popcorn and sodas. The movie was good even though it was about a girl. Well, at least she wasn't a foo-foo princess. Even Avery and Daichi liked it. As it ended there was a knock on the theater door. A White House staffer announced it was time to wash up for dinner. Sasha and I looked at each other, then down at our bloated stomachs. We were full of popcorn and now we had to eat dinner. We shrugged our shoulders and went to the private family quarters. There were clothes laid out for each of us and we were expected to wash up and all be ready in forty-five minutes. First Lady Michelle came in and officially told us we could call her Michelle. I asked her if I could call her Ms. Michelle and she said that was just fine. As she made sure Sasha's hair was "still in place." Sasha protested. Ms. Michelle gave her that mom look. Sasha silently sulked.

"Is this what you do every time at dinner?" I asked Sasha who said, "No, only if we are having dinner in the dining room with guests. Most of the time Malia and I eat with Mom and Dad in our family dining room. Of course, we do have to wash our hands."

Avery asked Ms. Michelle if our parents would be there. Ms. Michelle said yes that they were freshening up for dinner too after their long flight from California. My heart leapt with joy. I missed my parents so bad it hurt. I wondered out loud if the twins were here too. Ms. Michelle answered me saying that my parents came alone. Daichi and Jules' parents and grandparents were here also.

When the four of us were freshened up and changed a staff member took us down a hall and to a room where our parents waited. The staff member announced that dinner would be served at seven and a staff member would escort us to the dining room. I ran and hugged my mom who had tears running down her cheeks. We didn't speak for what seemed an eternity. Then she said, "I am so happy you are safe." She then held me at arm's length as if she were determining if I was really there and if I was the same kid. Then she pulled me back into her arms. Kissing me on the top of my head. I didn't even try to squirm away like I normally would have.

Dad was hugging Avery and was saying the same things Mom did except in guy terms. Then we switched and I was getting knuckled on the top of my head and Avery was getting kissed on his cheek over and over, while Mom said repeatedly how proud she was that he took such good care of me. She also said she was happy he was okay, but I liked the part about me. It made me feel like I was most important.

Daichi and Jules were exchanging the same kind of reunion with their parents. Their grandmother greeted them with a formal bow to which each of them responded in like. Then she too pulled them close to her and wept as she said something in Japanese. Daichi and Jules responded to her in Japanese. I liked hearing them speak Japanese. It was so rhythmic, almost like they were singing a song.

My parents let us know that they had been privy to our part of the top-secret information and that is all they said. Whew, there is no way I could keep this from my mom. She knows when I am trying to hide something. There was a gentle tap on the door. It was Ms. Michelle. She made her greetings which included how thrilled she was to see us all reunited. Then she said that dinner was ready to be served and she urged us to come with a nod of her head and a forward motion of her hand. She stepped back from the doorway as we filed past her into the hall. Then she moved to the front to lead us to the formal dining room.

I realized my dad had on his funeral suit. It was his only suit. Mom had on a flowing summer dress she had worn to my cousin Olivia's wedding. I was proud of how they looked. Avery and I followed in our Polo shirts and khaki slacks. Daichi wore the same exact thing as Avery and I. Jules wore a conservative sleeveless lavender dress, something like Kate, as in Prince William and Kate, would wear. The high heels worn by the women clicked rhythmically as we walked down the hallway.

Finally, we were in the dining room. I was glad because my narrative on fashion had reached its limits. Food, now that was a subject I could speak for hours on end, and we spent hours eating. Each portion was served on a separate plate. My friend Brooke would like that she had a fit if any of her food mixed and she refused to eat it. I mean nothing could make her eat it.

The servers made their way around the table with carts that had two or three choices of meat, bread, vegetables, (there were the most choices of veggies) and potatoes. I chose to have an extra helping of corn instead of a potato, eating a potato just didn't feel right, even though I knew they weren't Potahs. Anyway, corn is a starch. Dessert was served after everyone had finished eating. They were served on small plates so after getting a nod of okay from my mom I picked cheesecake and chocolate cake. With this we were served the coldest, most refreshing milk I had ever tasted. I could feel the coolness as it journeyed down to my stomach.

After being seated I scanned the room. I noticed Jules looking around, too. Avery was talking to a woman on his left. Daichi was speaking with his grandfather in Japanese. They burst out in laughter. Covering their mouths with their hands the sound was muffled. Grandfather was always making jokes that Daichi or Jules would translate to us. Sometimes the humor was lost in the translation. But the spirit was light.

The adults sipped coffee as they talked. Sasha asked her father if we kids could be excused to watch a movie. The President looked over at Ms. Michelle who nodded. Then the President said that she needed to excuse herself properly. Sasha stood up and thanked everyone for the fine company at dinner and thanked the staff for their service.

She waited until each of us did the same. When the last word was spoken, we left the room as quickly as we could without running. We gathered in the hallway far enough away from the dining room that we couldn't be heard.

"What movie do you want to watch?" Malia asked.

"Do you really want to watch a movie?" Sasha asked. Malia looked at her with a glance that could be translated as "here we go again."

"Sasha, you told Dad that we were going to watch a movie and that is what we are going to do." Malia insisted. The Secret Service agents stood nearby waiting for the outcome of the conversation.

Sasha looked at the agents. They would have to call in the change of location if Sasha won. Then her dad would know because his agent would tell him.

"Okay, how about the *Continental Divide*, you know the *Ice Age* movie?" She asked in a tone indicating the decision had been made. We nodded in agreement. This time there would be no popcorn. None of us could fit one more bite of anything into our stomachs.

CHAPTER 9

TRUTH OR FICTION

The next morning after breakfast on the patio looking over the Rose Garden, Avery got up the nerve to ask the President if the four of us could meet with him. He said, "Sure," and began to lead us to the Oval Office. Before we took a step I asked if our moms and dads could come, too. The President stopped and said of course. He sent an agent to invite them to come with us.

The four of them joined us in the Oval Office. Saying the Oval Office is as much fun as saying "debriefing." I mean when else in my life can I say either word? The setup of the room hadn't changed. We four kids sat on one couch and my mom, dad and Jules and Daichi's parents sat across from us and the President pulled up one of the two chairs from along the wall.

"Now, what is on your minds?" President Obama asked, genuinely interested.

I waited for one of the others to speak and no one did. Jules and I looked at each other. I nodded to her and she began to speak.

"With all due respect," she started, "I, um, we would like to know what is going on with the Second, I mean the Potah and well I mean what are the plans? I mean, where will the Second be once the interroga… interviews are over?"

"Those are excellent questions," President Obama replied, sounding like a politician.

I couldn't stop myself, I blurted out, "Can we have some excellent answers? I mean, Mr. President, will you be able to answer our questions?" My face turned beet red and the parents turned their eyes toward me and the others looked at me with disbelief.

"I apologize for Joshie." My mom said, as she shot me a "mom look."

President Obama smiled. "I think we have a future reporter." Everyone breathed a sigh of relief.

"Well, to answer the questions I am certain everyone in this room has, the investigation regarding the Potah has been completed. He is not considered a security risk at this time. The issue we are concerned with is whether or not to go public with this. We have evidence that militant Potahs pose a risk for the Potahs." He took a deep breath, "Since this Potah has made it to the topsoil others may follow. We have information from a source that there may be an influx of Potahs defecting and the threat of the rebels attacking."

"You knew about the Potahs?" Avery asked.

"We have had them under surveillance for a while." The President responded.

"Did your people have anything to do with that sinkhole that swallowed our children?" Daichi and Jules' mother asked in an accusing tone.

"We did not know until the implosion that they were readying for an infiltration from the center of the earth," The President continued, "When we learned that the kids were involved, we had to act strategically so they would not come into harm's way."

What we weren't told at this time was that the One and Two were spies for the government, the U.S. government. We weren't told because it would put the other resistors in jeopardy.

"Currently the Potah is resting in the finest soil. Being watered with the purest waters." President Obama assured us.

"What about the genetically altered fries that the wicked Potahs have been trading regular fries with?" Avery asked.

"We have been tracking those fries and that is why Michelle has launched the campaign to eat alternatives to fries. We have seen the results of the altered fries in our population. We have seen an alarming increase in the effects. Couch potatoes, humans genetically altered. The Potahs are attempting to render us helpless to an attack. Their goal is for we humans not to be able to get off our couches to defend ourselves." President Obama shared this top-secret information with us.

"May we ask how the government was able to recruit spies?" My dad asked.

"The Potahs are divided into two groups. Those who are set on revenge upon humanity for the Irish Famine, what they refer to as genocide." President Obama looked at each of us and then continued, "There are others that realize we are generations removed from the people that committed the horrendous acts against them. They want peace so the Top Siders and the Core Dwellers can work together for the best of our planet."

"So, what does all of this mean for the Second? Will the rebels come after him?" Daichi asked, the rest of us nodded in approval of his question.

"We feel that the Second can be safe as long as his identity is kept secret." There was a pause. "We are working on solutions that would do just that." I smiled. It was the first time that the President had referred to the Second by our nickname for him.

"Can we see the Second?" I asked hopefully.

"I can arrange that," The President said as he looked at the closest of the three agents standing by the doors and the windows. I wondered if the agents ever cut loose and smiled. Sasha had told me no. She tried. They have to always be ready to defend the first family and I guess they couldn't do that with a smile on their face. The agent exited. After a few minutes one of the other agents came to the President and simply said, "It's a go."

The two agents in the room led us down to where the Second was being held. We passed by cells that held half human and half Potahs. Some had human arms and legs, others had morphed further and were sprouting cable eyes. "Wha?" I turned to Avery who urged me to keep going. I resisted a little but was pushed forward by Jules who looked as spooked as I was.

Finally, we came to the room where our Potah was. He was in a noise proof, sealed lab with people in white coats with paper gowns and shoe covers. We had to wear the same thing, well, except the white coats. A curtain was drawn back, and we saw the Second sitting in a thick plot of soil with an IV of pure water dripping into him. One of his sides was missing a portion of starchy flesh. A bandage covered where a cable had been amputated. His arms were taped to his sides. He was in an unconscious state. He didn't know we were there.

"Here is our guest," One of the white coats said as we were ushered into the room.

"Guest! This is how you treat guests?" I said boldly. No one hushed me.

"You remember when you first came back, we took blood samples from each of you and gave you a thorough physical?" One of the white coats said.

"Yeah, but you didn't take flesh from us or cut off our eyes." Jules spoke courageously. No one hushed her either.

"Oh, and what is going on with the half human half Potahs we saw on the way in?" Avery spoke before I had a chance. I added, "Yeah, what is that about?"

Now my mom tugged on our shirts, signaling us to back down a little.

"The President will have to authorize us speaking to you about them." One of the white coats said, turning his attention to President Obama who responded with a nod of his head. The white coat raised his eyebrows in a silent questioning of the President.

"Go ahead," President Obama said.

"The ones you saw as you came in are the result of the French fry alterations. These are human's whose genetic code is changing them into Potahs. We are force feeding them salads and fruit. It is working on a couple of them. Once the process is finished, they cannot remember anything about being human. We have found hordes of them in the forest burrowed up to their arms in the rich moist soil. All they will say is, "They will come for us." The ones we have found so far are under twenty-four hour a day guard. They are in Leavenworth, the military prison. ``

"We took the cable eye and biopsies of this Potah to hopefully find a clue to restoring those affected." The first of the white coats disclosed.

"What will happen to our Potah?" Daichi asked.

"We are thinking that he can win the favor of those in Leavenworth and become a leader that has humanity's best interests in mind." President Obama interjected. "You know him the best, do you think he could be effective as a leader?" The question was directed at none of us and all of us.

We looked at each other. They had saved our lives but, as leaders we could not be sure. They led us, but we were willing followers. The four of us kids spoke amongst ourselves. We picked Jules to talk.

"Before the Potah can be effective as a leader, I think it's also necessary to consider what would be best for the Potahs and humanity." After assessing that her audience was engaged, Jules went on, "We need to learn what they need and how we can meet the needs of everyone while respecting each other's experiences. We need to accept them and be open to change that is best for all. For this to be successful we have so much to consider. The most important thing is we need to consider the Potahs as fellow Earthlings and recognize what is working for us, global unit and what needs to be revised or even reconstructed."

The adults stood gazing in wonder as they processed the words Jules had spoken. My dad started to say something. I blurted out in support of Jules, "You sound like Martin Luther King!" I saw the adults nod in agreement.

"Acceptance will lead to harmony," Jules added in a soft voice.

President Obama cleared his throat and said, "It is urgent before the others come that the Potah be a part of the solution. You are right, it does us no good if the Potah has no trust in us. Two risked his life for the four of you and One gave her life for you. I will give my endorsement that Two stays with you at a yet to be disclosed place while acceptance is worked on." The President paused for a moment and then continued. Turning his attention to our parents, "You will have to relocate if this is to take place. The U.S. government would take care of all expenses and provide leadership classes for the Potah. Of course, this will have to be approved by the Joint Chiefs of Staff. First, parents, I need your endorsement of the plan."

We turned and looked at our parents, pleading like we did when we wanted to take in a stray pet, even promising to take care of the Second's every need.

Daichi's dad spoke up, "It would be an honor to assist in the security of our nation."

Daichi's mom smiled and gently patted his father's arm, adding, "And the process of social and policy reform."

My mom and dad agreed. "Can grandpa come? What about Kiera and Jason, Jody, Jaden, Hayes, Eddie and Kyla? Ruby and Andrew and...." I was cut off at that point.

"As long as the Potah's are not discovered you can have your family come visit."

The President excused himself and we followed him out. He headed in the opposite direction than we did. We went up to the Rose Garden Terrace to have brunch. It was the best buffet I ever had. In about an hour the President came and asked for us to come with him.

We went to THE OVAL OFFICE. I capitalized it because it would probably be the last time I would get to say it. The President smiled and sat on the edge of his desk. He asked, "How was brunch?" Taking note of our exasperation he chuckled. "I suppose you want me to tell you the outcome of the meeting?" He chuckled again.

"Okay, seriously, the plan of the Potah living with your two families has been approved. We discussed different locations. The first one we discussed was Venice Beach because there are so many, um, unique things happening there no one would notice an overgrown potato. Then we thought of the Northwest. You know where Bigfoot has been spotted. We also considered Wrightwood, since they have done such, a great job integrating and protecting Auggie the Dragon. We decided on the Seattle region in a small town called Granite Falls. The mayor of Wrightwood will lead the integration process, working with the people in Granite Falls. The cottage we have chosen is just outside Granite Falls. It is in the mountains just above Granite Falls, right on the Rogue River. We figured if anyone spotted the Second, they would just consider him to be another type of Bigfoot, and since the Potah has big feet, it just seemed to fit. There is a cellar with mounds of soil and a water source for the Potah to stay, to sleep, and to avoid any visitors that may come."

So that is how I came to live with a giant potato. I work closely with Ms. Michelle on the war against genetically altered French fry awareness. The Second is taking an online leadership training. He uses Dragon Speaks to record his answers since his fingers are too thick for the keyboard. Once that is done, he will go to a leadership class that we four kids get to attend also. Then we will spend time with the humans turned Potah at Leavenworth to convince them that the Second represents the Potahs they have been waiting for.

Oh, and we don't eat any potatoes anymore, out of respect for the Potah.

"Joshua Durbin, is your homework done?" Mom yelled from downstairs.

"Um, yeah Mom, I mean yes, just now." I hollered back.

"Hurry up, dinner is almost ready!" She responded.

"On my way!" I shouted, closing my homework journal.

www.ingramcontent.com/pod-product-compliance
Lightning Source LLC
Chambersburg PA
CBHW031034190726
48286CB00003BA/1162